## NO WAY OUT . . .

He lingered a moment, and then turned abruptly to his door. There was no light in his room, and he left the door partly open till he could scratch a match and touch it to a lamp. As he did so, the door was gently shut, and he found himself standing between two men, each with his back to one of the doors. One held a cocked revolver. The other poised a feathered throwing knife.

The man near the hall door opened it, glanced into the hall, and gestured with his head. The other, the man with the knife, whispered, "Follow him. One word and you're dead."

# The Treasure of Fan-Tan Flat

## WILLIAM O. TURNER

A BERKLEY MEDALLION BOOK
published by
BERKLEY PUBLISHING CORPORATION

This is a work of fiction. It was suggested by a legend, one of those vague, wild bits of western folklore of which you seldom hear the same version twice. No doubt, there is a scintilla of fact to it; some of the events may even have occurred somewhat as I have presented them. But Star City is a fictional town, and all the characters are products of my imagination.

William O. Turner

SBN 425-03525-1

BERKLEY MEDALLION BOOKS are published by
Berkley Publishing Corporation
200 Madison Avenue
New York, N.Y. 10016

BERKLEY MEDALLION BOOK ® TM 757,375

Printed in the United States of America

Berkley Medallion Edition, JANUARY, 1978

# ONE

Steve Tanager first saw her from a poker table in the rambling room that was lobby, casino, and dining room of the Frontier House in Ogden, Utah Territory. It was on a hot June evening of 1874. She was slender and dark-eyed, and she moved through the garble of rude furniture with an unstudied majesty of bearing. Carriage, manner, poise— call it what you would—she had the subtle quality that is the difference between a truly beautiful woman and a merely pretty one. She had it without trying, had it forever; Steve knew this with certainty and knew it at a glance.

*A princess*, he thought. *A housewife or schoolteacher or maybe some manner of high-class tart, but a princess nonetheless*. He was gawking now, he realized. *Damn damnation!* he thought, *Gainsborough would have gawked, too*.

She put down her suitcase at the deserted registration desk and touched the bell with a gloved hand. Turning she cast a look around the room, a look that reached Steve's table as completely casual. There it changed to a quick little frown, and she immediately turned her back.

Steve's eyes swept the other four players. It seemed to him that she had recognized one of them, but they were all intent on the game and none gave any sign of noticing her. He threw in his tens and treys and studied the woman from the rear.

Her dark hair was done in a neat bun below a little pancake of a hat that was pinned in place. Her gray, ankle-length skirt showed no wrinkles. There was no trace of U.P. soot on the fringe of white lace above her coat collar. Still, she must have arrived on the five-thirty train, Steve concluded, the west-bound.

The oafish, shaggy-haired man called Slim Wiggins spread three queens and, as Steve expected, won the hand. It had been Wiggins' deal. Bald little Chancey Duncan slapped down his cards untidily.

"If luck was skunk juice, I'd smell like a rose," Chancey asserted bitterly.

Wiggins replied with a yellow-toothed grin and reached for his winnings. He wore an outlandish checked suit and a brown derby that sat on his mass of straw-colored hair like a hen on a nest. He encouraged the impression that he was fresh from an Iowa farm, but the deft and slender hands that swept in the pot showed no sign of what is usually thought of as work. The hands swiftly began to stack the chips; then they fell flat on the table as Wiggins looked up and saw the woman.

The desk clerk had appeared, had smiled for the first time that day, and had handed her a pen. As she signed the register, the clerk darted around the desk and picked up her suitcase. Raising a hand to her face and turning away

2

from the poker game, she followed him toward the stairs at the rear of the room.

Wiggins was on his feet. He pushed his chips toward the backsliding Mormon who was banking the game.

"Cash 'em. Count fair now."

Chancey Duncan was gathering the deck. He said, "Another hand, Wiggins."

"My kindest apologies, gents," Wiggins said, "but I got business."

He swaggered across the room and intercepted the woman at the foot of the stairs, snatching off his derby and making a clownish little bow.

"Mrs. Allison. This here is a unexpected surprise."

She neither spoke nor smiled. Wiggins inched closer and spoke in a lowered voice. She tried to go around him, but he side-stepped to block her. He was talking rapidly, smirking, gesturing with the derby. The clerk had gone on up the stairs.

She reached up and removed her own hat then, drawing the six-inch pin that held it to her hair. She looked Wiggins squarely in the eye and moved toward him, not quickly but with the hatpin aimed at his middle. He stepped back reflexively, then buckjumped out of her way. Muttering through clenched teeth, he watched her climb the steps. He seemed on the verge of following but did not. He clamped his hat on his head and swaggered back to the table. Soberly he counted his cash.

"You gents want another try at me, I'll likely be around later tonight."

"A wise decision," Steve said. "It's somebody else's night to be lucky at love."

"Love?" The word had a curious sound on the lips of this ugly, uncouth man. He seemed to realize for the first

3

time what a fool he had looked. "You misreckon, Major. I got business dealings with that little she-kitty."

Chancey Duncan pursed his lips and nodded his bald head. Only his eyes smiled. "Looked from here like you were going to get yourself a jeweled belly button."

The others laughed, and Wiggins grinned yellowly. "I caught her unexpected is all. She'll parley with me, all right, when she's had time to think things over."

The clerk came downstairs and began to sort mail at the desk. Wiggins stuffed his coin and greenbacks into a purse and strolled over, engaging the man in tense, subdued conversation. He had taken most of the money out of the game and the play dulled. After a few hands, the other players agreed to meet later and adjourned for supper.

Steve and Chancey crossed the street to a restaurant in one of the town's new adobe buildings. The food was starchy Mormon fare, but better than what the Frontier House served. Chancey, a huge eater for a small man, devoted himself to it with a singleness of purpose that discouraged conversation.

Steve couldn't get the woman out of his mind. Even if he never saw her again, he thought, she had a meaning for him, and he struggled to define it. There was always an omen that marked a change in your luck, he decided, and perhaps that's what she was—an omen.

He was becoming unable to think except in terms of the Game, he realized. He supposed he should be alarmed about this, but he was not. That was the insidious thing about the Game—you accepted its hold on you without challenge. Slowly but as surely as dope or booze, it took you over. It became *you*.

Damn damnation, how long had it been? How long had he been searching boats and trains and boom towns for the table that would make his fortune? Two years? Three? And now, in this little Mormon crossroads that had blustered into importance with the coming of the railroad, he was down to his bottom fifty dollars. It was time to quit, once and forever. But he knew that if he lost tonight, he would quit only long enough to raise another stake. The Game had taken him over, all right, but how had it happened? How?

The answer was tortuous and unsimple, but the sight of that woman had stirred up an impulse to take stock of himself . . . The war. Surely the answer was rooted in the war . . .

He had tasted glory at Cedar Mountain and Manassas— glory and terror and disgust. At Gettysburg, he had tasted Yankee grapeshot. There had been the lethal stench of a Union hospital then, and the wind-rasped hell of a prison camp on an island in Lake Erie. When at last he had returned to freedom, he had found it bitter and empty. He had beaten a carpetbagging politician to within an inch of his life, and he had had to flee Virginia.

That was the beginning of the years of wandering, the futile efforts to give direction to his life. There had been a command in a jungle revolution in Central America, the broken dream of a cattle empire in New Mexico, an ill-fated freighting venture in California. And then at last he had lost himself in the Game, where desire focused easily in greedy symbols. Money became the Principle of Everything; you knew perdition and salvation daily as you lost and won. Other needs faded. You knew no friends— opponents, partners, acquaintances; but not friends.

Chancey was no exception. Steve had known him casually last year on the river and had run into him here two days ago, quite by chance. Finding that they had a common enemy at the card table, they had been drawn together; but that didn't make him a friend.

Now in a mood to talk, Chancey shoved a cigar across the table and bit off the end of another.

"The barnyard wonder—how do you figure him, Major?"

"Wiggins?" Steve said. "A phenomenon. A dolt who has managed to give his hands a remarkable education."

"You know he's fancy-fingering us?"

"I'd have to guess," Steve admitted. "I've watched him like a hawk and detected nothing."

"Notice the calluses on his left hand?"

"Calluses? I'd say he has the hands of a virtuoso."

"There are two tiny ones," Chancey said. "One is at the base of his left thumb, the other near the tip of his third finger. They tag him as a bottom dealer."

Chancey explained how a bottom dealer holds the deck and how he buckles back the bottom card and kicks it into dealing position with his third finger.

"What can we do about it?" Steve asked.

"I have no conscience about slicking a slicker. I'm for cold-decking him. Tonight."

Steve shifted his big frame and reached for the cigar Chancey had placed on the table. He sliced off the tip with a penknife and flicked it away. The ethical nicety involved in slicking a slicker was unimportant, he decided.

"Can we get away with it?"

Chancey nodded. He was in his early thirties, but his bald head made him seem old and wise. "I know a good way of switching decks. Takes two to do it, but it's easy enough. I can teach you in a few minutes."

Steve scratched a sulphur match on his boot, held it at

arm's length till it was through sputtering, and then lighted the cigar.

"Fair enough," he said.

They found a small store where they could buy playing cards with the same back design as those sold at the Frontier House. They bought two decks, then went up to Chancey's room.

They sat side by side at a small table, and Chancey demonstrated the switch of decks. It was simple enough, depending on timing and naturalness of manner rather than special skill. Steve sat at the left of Chancey, the dealer. As Chancey placed the cards to his right to be cut, Steve sneaked the stacked deck onto Chancey's knee. Chancey took the fair deck in dealing position in his left hand. As he leaned forward to ante, he dropped that hand below the edge of the table for a scant second—during which he laid the deck in Steve's palm and immediately grasped the stacked one. The moves were bold but swift and uncomplicated, and the business of anteing distracted attention.

Soberly, they ran through the routine several times.

"To do this during a game is going to take a special kind of nerve," Steve said.

Chancey chuckled. "You've never indulged in this sort of thing before?"

The question struck Steve as impudent; it was as if Chancey saw him as making a moral compromise and was enjoying it. Steve bit back a brusque reply.

"Poker is dog eat dog," he said. "It's just that I'd rather let others do the sharping."

"Very upright. And expensive."

"It's neither," Steve said. "Suppose a man runs in a

marked deck. You know it, but he doesn't know you know it. That gives you a considerable advantage. Or you sit to the right of a man who crimps the deck in an effort to make you cut where he wants. Cut one card below the crimp and you'll get the hand he has stacked for himself."

Chancey pursed his lips. "Never thought of that. And I suppose—"

He broke off as someone tapped on the door of the next room. A muffled voice said, "I know you're in there, Mrs. Allison."

They listened. The tapping was repeated. After a long moment, a key turned in the lock and the door opened. A woman said, "Five minutes. No longer."

"That's Wiggins!" Chancey said. "And the lady of the hatpin."

"I'm damned," Steve said. "She's let that clown in."

Raising a finger to his lips, Chancey stepped silently to the wall and pressed an ear against it. Steve could hear the murmur of voices and was tempted to go to the wall and listen, too, but did not. For some minutes, he sat toying with the cards; then he heard the door open and voices in the hall again. Chancey came back to the table.

"What's going on?" Steve said.

"Couldn't get it all," Chancey said softly. "Wiggins was declaring himself in on something or other. She didn't like it much." He picked up one of the decks and wove the ends together in a faro shuffle. "Seems that the lady is taking the morning stage for Star City. Ever been there?"

"Never," Steve said.

"Hell of a trip. Five days right up the spine of the Rockies."

"Wiggins is going, too?"

Chancey threw him a quick, piercing glance; then he

nodded. "I gather that he's going on horseback . . . Let's try that switch again." He sat down.

"What're they up to?" Steve said.

"Ha! The major smells money. Money and a beautiful woman, Major—that's a fatal combination. Myself, I'm too young to die."

Steve laughed mirthlessly. Chancey ribbon-spread a deck on the table and began picking out cards, stacking hands.

"Hope we can corner that rooster before he leaves town," Chancey said. "We'll deal him a small full, and you'll beat him with jacks up . . ."

# TWO

Susan Allison closed the door behind Slim Wiggins and quickly turned the key in the lock. Exasperated, she sat down on the bed, a hand raised to her eyes. What a sly, repugnant, insinuating man he was! And she had made a deal with him!

There was no other way, of course. Offering him ten per cent of the money was the only possible way to keep him from hounding her to death—and ruining her plans in the bargain. And she did need somebody to buy that property for her, somebody who would seem to be acting entirely on his own.

The trouble was that Wiggins obviously had no intention of taking only ten per cent. Accepting her proposition had been merely a way to get a finger into the pie. In his smirking, half-fawning, half-threatening way, he had made it plain that he meant to get both hands into it, up to the elbows.

The worst of it was there might be others like him before

she was through. She meant to keep to herself in Star City, but in all probability she would be recognized there. Star City might very well abound with Wigginses.

For just a moment she felt an urge to fling herself prone and sob her inadequacy to the coarse linen bedspread, but she had long ago ruled such indulgences out of her life. Tears were for the weak; they augured failure. Now as never before, she had to be strong—and shrewd. This journey to Star City was not a thing that she had wanted, and she dreaded it with all her being. How many times had she sworn she would never, never go back? But now she was doing it, and she was going to go through with it without weakness or indecision. She would somehow find a way to protect herself against the Wigginses of the world. When it was all over, when she had the money and was safely back in Iowa, she could remember this dark and frightened moment and cry if she wanted to.

She crossed to the cheap, white-framed mirror over her washstand and confronted an elongated version of her face that made her smile. She had had no supper and she decided that food would make her feel better. She readjusted a hairpin, put on her jacket, and went downstairs.

It was after eight by the clock over the registration desk. The only diners were a quartet of bullwhackers with the grime of the road still on their faces. At other tables, men were playing cards. Slim Wiggins was in a game with two of the men he had been playing with earlier—both, to judge by the square cut of their beards, were aberrant Mormons. To Susan's relief, Wiggins didn't even glance at her.

She selected a table in a corner and sat down. A Kanaka waiter explained in broken English that she would have to be content with stew and dumplings, and she smiled her acquiescence. While she was eating, a dapper little man and a tall, powerfully built man joined Wiggins' table, and Susan recalled that they had also been in the earlier game.

Briefly, her eyes met those of the big man and there was a communication in the look that frightened her. There was the need and the challenge she had seen ten thousand times in the eyes of men; but there was something more—a reflection of these in herself so stark and involuntary that she quickly looked down at her plate.

He sat down between Wiggins and the little bald man. Disturbed, Susan studied his profile. He had handsome dark hair with a gentle wave to it. His face might have been called handsome, too, if it weren't for the broken nose and the small star-shaped scar that splashed his cheek. She could catch a scrap or two of talk from the table, and she gathered that he was called Major Tanager. She was not good at guessing ages, but she judged him to be somewhere under thirty-five.

Chiding herself for behaving like a schoolgirl, she tried to concentrate on the tasteless stew. It was being tired and alone, she decided, that caused her to be intrigued by the mere sight of a strong man. *Strength*, she thought. Strength was what she needed more than anything else on earth.

A tense hand was being played at the table now. It narrowed down to a contest between Wiggins and one of the Mormons, and they raised each other again and again. Finally, Wiggins won.

Susan asked the waiter to bring more coffee. She had to catch the stage in the morning and she needed rest; but for some unclear reason she wanted to sit in this smoke-smeared room and surreptitiously watch a card game. She sipped the coffee and watched. The deal had gotten around to the bald man when the game exploded—more or less literally.

Without warning, Wiggins flung his right arm against Major Tanager's throat in a swift, sweeping motion that brought Wiggins to his feet and toppled the major over backward in a shower of playing cards. As if by magic, Wiggins held a small revolver, which he cocked as the major untangled himself from his chair and got to his feet.

"He's a cheat!" Wiggins' voice was shrill with indignation. "He had another deck in his lap."

"You're a liar," the bald man said calmly. He was still holding the deck he had been dealing.

Wiggins gestured wildly. "The proof is all over the place!"

"You had those cards in your hand," the bald man said.

Men all over the room had come to their feet, craning their necks but not leaving their tables. The Kanaka waiter backed into Susan's chair, gave her a wide-eyed look as if she had been stalking him from behind, and fled toward the kitchen. The clerk came from behind the desk with a billy club in hand and circled the fracas in a hesitant dance.

"Now, now, now," he kept saying. "Now, now, now! The Saints will fine us all."

"This here man is a dishonest card-cheat," Wiggins asserted, his voice quavering with righteousness.

The bald man stood up. Wiggins took a hasty step backward so as to cover him as well as the major with the gun.

"Keep out of this, Chancey," Major Tanager said.

He was smiling ever so slightly. He had survived being spilled over backward with no more lack of poise than if he had merely taken part in some strenuous party stunt. He was actually enjoying himself, Susan thought.

13

He moved toward Wiggins without haste, apparently confident that the man wouldn't shoot. Then with a light-ninglike crisscrossing of his hands, he had the revolver away from Wiggins and had an armlock on him to boot. He calmly took an instant to lower the hammer of the gun, and precisely, rather gently, he rapped Wiggins over the ear with it.

Wiggins collapsed like a grotesque rag doll. The major tossed the weapon to the bald man, who caught it and slipped it into a pocket. The two of them lifted Wiggins to his feet and lowered him into his chair, where he fought for consciousness, mouth open, head rolling crazily. The major picked up his own chair, sat down in it, and addressed himself to the two Mormon players, neither of whom had stirred.

"Mr. Wiggins is correct, gentlemen. I did have another deck in my lap, and you are entitled to an explanation. Wiggins has been sharping this game for two days. I meant to get back at him."

The two Mormons looked at each other. The bald man sat down and said something Susan didn't catch. A hushed conference followed. The clerk returned to the desk. Men at other tables resumed their games. Wiggins started to rise from his chair, but the major shoved him back into it. After that, Wiggins sat still with his head in his hands.

Susan rummaged through her bag for a scrap of paper and a pencil. Her fingers were shaking with excitement, not as the result of witnessing a poker-game brawl but because she had made an amazing decision. All reason, all common sense was against her; yet, intuitively, she was sure of herself. She wrote briefly, folded the paper, and looked around for the waiter, who was standing near the kitchen door. She signalled him, paid for her meal, and handed him the note.

"Wait till I've gone upstairs. Then give this to Major Tanager," she said quietly.

She spent the next few minutes tidying her room, pushing her unpacked suitcase under the bed, arranging two chairs so that the length of the room was between them. After the briefest of rituals in front of her mirror, she sat down to wait. She had expected the major to appear promptly, and she found herself annoyed when he did not. She had about given him up when the soft knock came. She took a deep breath and called, "Come in."

Major Tanager swung open the door. He smiled and nodded politely but didn't cross the threshold until he had swept the room with his eyes. He left the door open behind him, and she got up to close it.

"I'm Susan Allison," she said. "I saw that fuss downstairs."

"I'm sorry," he said.

"Please sit down." She gestured toward a chair and sat down in the other one. He sat down on the bed. She folded her hands in her lap and spoke words that sounded silly as soon as they were out.

"I suppose you are the sort of man who sometimes gets invitations from women who are—romantically inclined. I want to make it clear—"

"Seldom," he said. "And never from *beautiful* women, Mrs. Allison."

"Well—" She was mildly disconcerted. "I want to make it clear that I asked you here to discuss a business matter."

"The beautiful ones always want to discuss business."

15

"Really?" she said crisply, rejecting his flippancy. "I'll get to the point. From what I saw downstairs, I have the impression that you are perhaps a little desperate—financially speaking. Otherwise, I wouldn't have the nerve to make the offer I have in mind. You see, I need a sort of bodyguard."

He was startled—and interested. "A *sort* of bodyguard?"

"I don't know what else to call it," she said. "You see, I'm leaving for Star City on the morning stage. I haven't been there for a number of years; but if I'm recognized, I'll probably have enemies there. Also, I expect to bring back a considerable amount of cash."

He took a moment to consider this, squinting upward at nothing. She waited primly.

"And so you need the protection of a strong and reliable man," he said finally.

"That's about it, Major Tanager."

"And I strike you as reliable?" Their eyes met, and he smiled slightly.

"Up to a point—beyond which I'll try not to push you."

"Exactly what is your proposition?" he said.

"You accompany me to Star City and back. I'll pay you fifty dollars a week, plus expenses and a five-hundred-dollar bonus when you deliver me and the money safely here in Ogden. That should make you a nice little stake, Major."

"About this money you're going after." He was studying her intently now. "Whose is it?"

"My claim to it is better than most."

"That doesn't tell me much."

16

"I'm not going to tell you much. You're simply to come along and do exactly as I say."

"I see," he said. "You're putting the least possible strain on my somewhat doubtful reliability."

"For the time being."

"I don't see why you picked me. You could have got some nice Mormon with a shotgun. And for less money."

"I acted on an impulse when I saw how easily you handled Mr. Wiggins. You see, he's in this, too. Alone, I couldn't keep him under control. You can."

"I'd like to know more about Mr. Wiggins," he said.

"He came originally from my county in Iowa. He also was in Star City eight years ago when I was there. He knows all about that part of my life and about this money I'm going after. He has been plaguing me to go back and get it—with his help, of course. I swore I would never go back. Now I need money desperately and I'm going. He must have got word—his cousin is the railroad-station agent at Cedar Rapids. Anyway, it's plain that Wiggins' being here to meet me is no accident."

"So you had to deal with him."

She sighed wearily. "If he were to tell what he knows about me, he could ruin me—and my family as well. He could also wreck my plans to get the money." She sighed again and added, "I do have a use for him, but I won't give him the half-share he wants. I promised him ten per cent."

Major Tanager nodded ever so slightly. He seemed vaguely amused. "I see. I'm to do exactly as I'm told, and I'm to see that Wiggins does the same."

"And to look out for my interests in general."

They let the silence drag a moment; then he grinned broadly, boyishly, and the hardness of his scarred face disappeared. He was handsome after all, Susan thought—and wished he weren't.

He said, "Common sense tells me I should make you a polite little bow and get out of here, Mrs. Allison. But common sense has never had much influence on my life, I'm sorry to say. I'll give the job a try."

"There's one more thing I must tell you," she said, speaking rapidly. "It's just possible that I can avoid being recognized at Star City. So I must attract as little attention as possible. As a woman traveling alone, I might attract a good deal."

She studied him to see if he anticipated what she was going to propose. He gave no sign that he did.

"Traveling with a bodyguard will be even worse," she said. She was trying to be crisp and businesslike. "The sensible thing is to pretend to be husband and wife."

He looked away thoughtfully, showing no surprise. "Very sensible."

She had the feeling that he might be inwardly amused and struggling not to show it. Suddenly she was embarrassed.

"I guess I put that badly," she said.

"Not at all," he said. Then he burst out, "Damn damnation, Mrs. Allison! Where in tunket is *Mr.* Allison?"

"You might as well get used to my first name," she said. "It's—"

"Susan."

"And yours is—?"

"Steve. Do you mind answering my question?"

"Mr. Allison is in Iowa. He knows nothing about—that is, he doesn't know my real reason for this trip."

The lie made her uncomfortable, but it seemed neces-

18

sary. He was watching her closely, and she wondered if he suspected that she did not have a husband at all. Poker players were supposed to be expert at reading faces.

"The stage leaves at five in the morning," she said. "Wiggins intends to leave around midnight, I believe. That is, if he wasn't hurt too badly."

"He wasn't."

They both stood up, and Susan found herself wishing she weren't dismissing him quite so quickly. There was a stiffness of manner between them that ought to be broken down if they were to pose as man and wife. At the door she briefly gave him her hand.

"Good night, Steve," she said.


Steve stopped at the stairway, counted twenty, and went back along the hall. Quietly passing Susan's doorway, he reached Chancey's and tapped lightly with a fingernail. The door opened at once, and Chancey jerked his head in invitation to come in.

"You hear all that?" Steve said softly.

"Most of it," Chancey's wrinkled forehead gave him the aspect of a worried puppy. "You're not really taking the hook?"

One of Chancey's ears was definitely redder than the other from being pressed against the wall. For all Steve knew, Susan might have her ear against the other side of it. The ridiculousness of the thought made him smile.

"There's a lot of money in this somewhere," he muttered.

"And a lot of woman?"

"Seems like it."

"And death," Chancey said. "A lot of death."

19

Steve was startled. "Wiggins?"

"You're going to have to kill him—unless he back-shoots you first."

"How do you figure that?"

Chancey shrugged. "It's plain enough. He means to take this woman for a sleigh ride, and you'll be in his way. On top of that, he isn't going to forget what you did to him tonight."

There was a stone bottle of Valley Tan on the dresser. Steve uncorked it and sniffed. "Damned if I see what you're so spooky about."

Chancey moved to the washstand and got two glasses. "A determined woman, that's what."

"She's got into something over her head, something she hates," Steve said.

"Sure. And she's trying to hire you to do the dirty work." Chancey took the bottle from Steve and poured three fingers of liquor for each of them. They clinked glasses.

"*Salud y dinero,*" Steve said.

"Miss that stage!" Chancey said.

He tossed down his drink. Steve sipped his, finding the Mormon liquor flavorless and scalding.

"They must dip this stuff out of that 'lake of fire' Brigham Young is always talking about," Chancey said, pouring himself another. "You know anything about Star City?"

"I've heard some of the legends about its wild days."

"They say it was the bloodiest town on the face of the earth till the vigilantes strung up Ben Roman and twenty-odd others."

"Ben Roman," Steve said. "He was a mining-district judge, wasn't he?"

Chancey nodded. "And head of the best-organized gang of cutthroats the West has ever seen. Not only did every road agent belong to it, but every sluice-robber, sneak thief, and drunk-roller. They all turned over a chunk of their take to the organization, and they had things their own way. They ran wild. I'm told there were over a hundred murders in the three-month period following the strike in Star Gulch."

"So the decent people formed a vigilance committee," Steve said. "What was the leader's name? Gaul, wasn't it—Tim Gaul?"

"Nobody suspected Ben Roman," Chancey went on. "He was a respected man, hobnobbed with the territorial governor. But the vigilantes rounded up some of the small fry, who named Roman in their confessions. And he confessed, himself, before he hanged."

Steve finished his drink and set down his glass. "How long ago was all this, Chancey?"

"Let's see—must've been about '66. The point is, Major, that the vigilante tradition still hangs heavy over the town. The courts are downright ruthless, I'm told. Remember that if you have to do in Wiggins—or one of those vague enemies the lady hinted at."

In his own room, Steve stripped, washed himself, laid out clean clothes for morning, packed his suitcase. When at last he got into bed, he was too stirred up to sleep for a while. He lay on his back, frowning in the darkness as he contemplated Susan.

She had said she left Star City eight years ago. That would put it in '66—the year of the vigilante cleanup, if Chancey's memory was correct. What had she meant by

21

that remark about having enemies if she should be recognized? Had she had something to do with the vigilantes? Or was it the Roman gang?

*It makes no difference*, he thought. *She's a princess, no matter what.*

He slept tensely, dreaming of the Game, misreading his cards, betting cinch hands that faded magically into losers, bucking a yellow-toothed monster of an opponent who was not a man but the Game itself. He woke to a persistent tapping on the door. Grumbling, he got out of bed and lighted a lamp. His watch read a quarter past midnight. Barefoot and in his underwear, he unlocked the door. He was confronted by Slim Wiggins, who grinned raggedly.

"Been talking to Mrs. Allison," Wiggins said. "She tells me you're in this here business proposition of ours. I come to forget past bygones and say welcome."

He came into the room and held out his hand. Steve hesitated, then took it.

"Nice of you," he said. "I thought you were to stay away from Mrs. Allison."

"We got to seem strangers in Star City, that's all. I'm leaving right away, ahorseback."

*"Bon voyage,"* Steve said. The man irritated him, and he could think of nothing else to say.

"The same to you . . . Mrs. Allison explained to me she's going to claim to be Mrs. Tanager."

"I'm glad she put it that way. I was afraid I was going to be Mr. Allison."

Wiggins regarded him sharply and lingered as if there were more to say. Steve was tempted to question him about Susan Allison but decided against it. Likely as not the real purpose of this visit was to learn how much—or how little—she had told Steve.

"Just wanted to bury the tomahawk, Major," Wiggins said. "No use of me and you bucking a grudge."

"No," Steve said.

At the door, Wiggins turned and gave Steve his hand again. Steve locked the door behind him, blew the lamp, and returned to his bed.

"Chancey is right," he muttered to his pillow. "I'm going to have to kill that rascal, sure as sin."

# THREE

The stage left Ogden as sunrise spilled over the Wasatch to give the barren land its interval of splendor. Stark ridges bloomed with creeping color. The road and the strip of desert between it and the great lake took on a soft rose cast that stained the dust devils. When the distant water could be glimpsed, it glistened blindingly, black-rimmed by its ragged shore. But within minutes it dulled to a sterile gray, and contrasts burned from the land to leave a parched monotony relieved only rarely by the green of an irrigated field or a cluster of cottonwoods around an adobe farmhouse.

It was already hot. And even with the coach windows wedged shut, the silken dust of the churned road tormented the five passengers. Susan and the other woman making the trip wore double-thick veils that covered their heads to their shoulders and gave them the look of beekeepers. The three men looped bandannas around their necks, and when the dust was thickest, drew them up over their noses. Conversation was thus severely hampered, tobacco had a harsh taste, dozing was difficult. For the most part, the passengers retreated into themselves for whatever anodyne to tedium they could find there.

The woman who rode beside Susan did try to chat at first, launching an account of her dead husband's accomplishments. Happily, she quickly went hoarse. The other passengers were a pleasant-faced Mormon businessman, who somehow appeared completely comfortable, and a youngish, slightly built man in a dove-gray riding coat of severe cut. He spoke not at all during the first hour, but he had a disconcerting way of staring intently at each of his fellow passengers in turn. When Steve finally prodded him into speech, he was surprised to discover that the man was a Mexican.

"I speak very poor the English," he said apologetically. "I learn it from a book, so I read pretty good but don't speak."

Steve grinned and asked in fluent if grammatically ragged Spanish what he was doing so far from home. Delighted, the man introduced himself as Carlos Ramirez y O'Brian, fresh from a remote part of Sonora. He had blue eyes, Steve noticed.

They talked for a time, with Ramirez reticently parrying questions about his business in Star City. Once, when the coach swayed unexpectedly, his coat fell open to expose the butt of a revolver in a shoulder holster. An instant later, as Ramirez buttoned the garment, Steve glimpsed the hooked handle of a derringer clipped to a wristlet under the Mexican's left sleeve. Whatever his errand, Ramirez was armed to the teeth.

After nearly three hours of travel, the stage entered a village and drew up at the stable to change horses. A bench along the outer wall of the building had been set with tin wash basins and buckets of cool water dipped from the ditch that brought it down from the mountains. Here the passengers eagerly bathed their faces and dried them on a roller towel of Mormon linen.

Steve and Susan strolled up the main street of the neat, typically Mormon town with its wide streets, large lots, and precise line of adobe houses. Susan carried her hat and veil in her hand; for a time they breathed deeply of the hot, clear air without speaking. When they turned to go back to the coach, she broke the silence.

"Did you notice the driver staring at me when I was washing my face? I think he recognized me."

Steve met her glance and saw that she was making an effort to speak casually.

"You know him?" he asked.

"His name is Jase Nooner. He used to own the stage line in the old days."

"Seems I've heard the name," Steve said, searching his memory.

"I think he was one of the vigilante leaders— although I'm not sure. I left Star City before the vigilantes took over."

A block away, the passengers were climbing back into the stagecoach. Susan quickened her step.

"There's plenty of time," Steve said. "I wish you'd tell me about the early days of Star City."

"They were wild and terrible," she said, staring straight ahead. "A killing every day. The Roman gang had the whole territory terrorized."

"And Susan Allison had it at her feet, I imagine."

"Hardly. And I wasn't Susan Allison then."

"Who were you?"

She touched him with an uneasy glance. "You haven't guessed?"

"No."

She let the silence drag. After a moment, he said, "It seems to me I'm bound to learn all about you sooner or later."

She stopped and faced him. "It isn't an easy thing to say. I was Susan Roman."

Her eyes bored into him, searching for his reaction. At the same time, there was a defiant tilt to her chin. He looked away.

"Mrs. Ben Roman?" he said.

"Yes."

"I see." He needed time to fit the fragments of the picture together. "Ben Roman hid some loot somewhere, and you're going after it?"

"It— Yes, I suppose it is loot."

"You know where it is?"

She nodded and moved on toward the coach, where the driver was climbing up to his seat. Steve caught her elbow and slowed her down.

"Why have you waited so long, Susan? Eight years!"

She hurried on without speaking for a moment. Then she said, "My husband was hanged. I was on my way back to Iowa when I heard about it. I hadn't the slightest suspicion he was a criminal. Can't you understand what the news did to me?"

"I suppose not," he said gently.

"I was on the verge of losing my mind. I had to live as if Star City didn't exist."

He wanted to touch her, to say he was sorry; but it seemed to him that any words he could find would sound shallow and perfunctory. And perhaps hypocritical as well. *There is a great deal of money*, he thought. *She knows where it is. That's the only thing that matters very much*.

The driver was staring down at them, and Susan put on her hat and veil. Steve handed her into the coach and climbed in after her.

By early afternoon they had eaten a warmed-over meal at an isolated way station, had crossed the Bear, and were following a twisting road along the east bank of the Malad. During the swaying, dust-beaten hours between stops, Steve tried to recall everything he had heard about the notorious Roman gang.

Up on the driver's seat, Jase Nooner was also thinking about Ben Roman, whom he had helped to hang. It had been one of the great satisfactions of Jase's life, for he blamed the gang for the failure of his stage line. They had somehow always known when his coaches carried gold, and they had robbed him blind. Unable to reimburse shippers for their losses, he had been forced out of business as soon as the Overland came to Star City. Wells Fargo had taken over the Overland and now had sold the line to Gilmer and Salisbury, for whom Jase was driving.

Before they strung up Ben Roman, they had questioned him about his loot. He had sworn that his lieutenant, Luke Lumby, had gotten out of the territory with it, and Jase had been inclined to believe him. At the time, the vigilantes still had hopes of catching up with Lumby. But he had never been seen or heard of since.

Today, for the first time in eight years, Jase was beginning to give credence to the rumors of buried treasure that had haunted Star City since Roman's execution. He was almost certain that the handsome Mrs. Tanager now in his coach and the shy, poke-bonneted girl who had married

Ben Roman were one and the same. And what purpose could she possibly have for returning to Star City except to recover money her husband had hidden? Jase could think of none other.

The more he mulled it over, the more his excitement—and his resentment—grew. If there was a treasure, a good share of it was rightly his. Legally speaking, he supposed that the gold the Roman gang had lifted from his stages belonged to the shippers, if they could be found. But an owner was entitled to something for his busted business, wasn't he? Enough to start a new line, at least.

Jase decided that he would plead a bad back and lay off driving for a while. He would stay in town and keep his eye on the Tanagers. Damn it, he wished that big, well-dressed, scar-faced major wasn't in the picture. He had a look about him Jase didn't like, and he was certainly no man to get into a showdown with. With just the woman to deal with, things would be easier.

The first thing to do, Jase decided, was to get friendly with the Tanagers. Maybe he ought to come right out and, polite as pie, tell her he remembered her. Then he could offer sympathy, information, or whatever else was needed to worm his way into their trust. Then . . .

He struggled with violent, half-formed plans, muttering to himself, letting his voice rise now and then as he hurled a vocable down to the horses. Taking a blind downgrade turn too fast, he suddenly overtook a rider and for a moment was in danger of piling up the team. As it turned out, the traveler maneuvered his tired horse against the bank just in time. The coach swayed out of the ruts precariously, and Jase was too busy staying on the seat to give more than a glance and a bit of Biblical language to the rider, a gaunt man in a checked suit and brown derby.

29

Under the derby, where Jase expected a face, there seemed to be a grinning death's-head. Jase knew it was an illusion, the result of the sideways glance, dust, and the skidding coach; but it shook him to his boots. On the next turn he held the horses to a slower pace, thinking that he had had a warning to be cautious in his driving—and maybe in his thinking, too.

By evening they were over the Idaho line. The road bored through timber, spun across wasted flats. Bleak buttes rose abruptly. Rocky canyons widened into grassy valleys. It was a country of contrasts and of a permeating unity, a wilderness suspended in something lovely and forlorn.

The sun died bloodily and the air was soon cool. Night came quickly to the valleys, while twilight lingered on the flats and ridges. At last, with the horses held to a walk in the darkness, the coach arrived at the way station where the passengers would spend the night.

The shabbiness of the interior of the long log building was in keeping with the unshaven appearance of the two youngish bachelors who ran it. It was larger than most stations, however, and one of the proprietors showed Steve and Susan to a bedroom they could have to themselves.

Susan laughed nervously. "Every stage station I've ever seen had only two sleeping rooms—one for men and one for women."

"Don't cost nothing extra," the stationkeeper said proudly. "Supper in five minutes."

He left them alone, dragging the leather-hinged door shut behind him. Susan regarded the iron bedstead doubtfully.

"I didn't anticipate this."

"No problem," Steve said. "I'll sleep on the floor."

She continued to study the bed. The faintest touch of roguishness crept into her voice. "It would seem odd if we asked to be separated. Do you snore?"

"Only when I sleep on the floor."

She looked at him with mock exasperation, then stepped to the room's small mirror and began to remove her hat. "In Star City we'll try to get adjoining rooms so we can both be comfortable."

Someone beat on a pan, and they went into the dining room. The other passengers were already there, seating themselves on benches at a crude board table. The meal consisted of antelope stew, doughy bread, coffee, and prune pie. It was badly cooked; but fourteen hours in a jolting coach had made everybody hungry, and the serving dishes were quickly emptied.

The food put Susan into a chatty mood, and she prodded the stationkeepers into small talk about the country and the isolated life they led. The other woman passenger, a bird-faced little creature of indeterminate age, recovered her voice and joined in. The Mormon businessman told a funny story which Steve translated into Spanish for Ramirez's benefit, and the evening began to take on an aura of gaiety.

Jase Nooner took no part in the talk; but after every bite, his eyes returned to Susan's face. She gave no sign of annoyance, but finally Steve could stand it no longer.

"Something wrong, Mr. Nooner?" he asked.

Jase gulped, startled with a mouthful of stew. "Wrong?"

"You keep staring at my wife," Steve said pleasantly. He felt Susan's swift glance.

It took Jase a moment to phrase a reply. When the words

came, they were heavier with insinuation than he meant them to be.

"It keeps comin' to me I seen her somewheres before."

There was something subtly threatening in Steve's small gesture of putting down his fork, but he grinned and reached for Susan's hand. "A dangerous observation to make about a beautiful woman, sir."

Jase grinned uneasily. "Thing like that pesters a man, that's all."

"You look familiar to me, too," Susan said impetuously.

"Star City, wasn't it?" Jase's eyes were touched with a glint of eagerness. "Back in '66?"

"Now, Mr. Nooner, you spoiled it by mentioning the date. You'll have me giving away my age."

"Would you believe she's older than I am?" Steve said to the table in general.

"I am not!" Susan protested. "Why I'm—I'm *years* younger!"

There was laughter, and the Mormon businessman remarked that Steve was given to dangerous observations himself. Jase seemed to have been effectively sidetracked. He finished his meal with his eyes on his plate.

When they were back in their room, Steve struck a match and stepped toward the lamp on the table.

"Don't light it for a moment," Susan said. She crossed to the one window in the room, a big, glassless square fitted with an inswinging shutter that now hung open. She stood with her hands on the sill and filled her lungs with the brisk night air.

Steve blew the match, and picking his way in the darkness, reached her side. They looked up at a brushy slope with starlight tingeing the scrub pine at its crest. It was not much of a view, but there was a piercing fascination in the night itself.

"The mountain night!" Susan said, a liquid note coming into her voice. "There's something haunting about it. Something as sweet as love and as frightening as death."

She shivered, and he slipped his arm around her. When he tried to draw her closer, she pulled away.

"You're not to touch me, Steve," she said quietly. "Not ever."

"Then you're not to stand in the darkness and speak of love and death."

He made his way back to the table and fumbled for another match.

"Steve! There's something out there. In the brush."

"Some animal," he said. "Maybe a coyote."

She turned away from the window as the lamp flared. "It's something large and slow-moving. Like a man."

He lighted a cigar from the lamp before he replaced the chimney. Susan banged the shutter closed but didn't fasten it. It swung wide open again as she crossed the room toward the bed.

"It gives me the feeling that we're being watched," she said.

She put her hands to her head and withdrew the pins that held her hair in a bun. As it tumbled to her shoulders, she tossed her head and made an effort to change her mood.

"As least, I don't want a man watching me go to bed. Will you go somewhere else for a few minutes?"

There was a scrape of heavy footsteps outside the door and a sharp knock. Steve swung it open and faced Jase Nooner.

"Thought we ought to have a word in private," Jase said, smiling uneasily as he came into the room.

"Fine," Susan said. "Sit down, Mr. Nooner."

Steve turned a chair out from the table, but Jase shook his head.

"After settin' that coach since sunup, standin' is downright restful." Jase went around the table to the window and stared into the night as if he needed a moment to phrase his thoughts.

"You're a good driver," Susan said pleasantly.

"That's no praise by my lights, ma'am. I owned this line once."

"Yes. I remember."

Jase turned to face her. "I remember you, too, ma'am —who you was and all. Can't help but wonder why you're goin' back."

"I have business in Star City," Steve said brusquely. "Susan came along for the trip."

Jase gave Steve the briefest of glances and leaned back with his elbows on the windowsill. Addressing himself to Susan, he said, "There ain't too many left who would recognize you—seeing how you've changed a bit and all. And I won't say a word, ma'am, if you'd like it that way."

"Naturally, I'd like it very much."

"Put your mind at rest then," Jase said. " 'Course, there's folks you ought to steer clear of. Tim Gaul—"

The crack of the rifle was not loud in the high, thin air. Simultaneously with it, Jase Nooner coughed and pitched forward into the table. Steve caught the lamp before it crashed. He immediately blew it and strode toward the window. On the way, he bumped into Susan. It wasn't till then that she screamed.

At the window, he tried to blink away the lingering image of the lamp flame. Just once, he saw motion in the brush that might have been a man climbing the slope.

34

There were footsteps at the door now, men stumbling into the room. One of the stationkeepers arrived with a lantern, and Steve closed the shutter.

Susan was bending over Jase Nooner. She looked up, scanning the pressing, peering faces till she found Steve's.

"He's dead," she said.

# FOUR

It was after midnight when Steve entered the bedroom to find blankets and a pillow laid out for him on the floor. Susan lay motionless in the bed with an arm flung over her face. She looked very small and childlike under the covers. Steve quietly pulled off his boots, blew out the low-burning lamp, and stretched out.

The shutter was closed, and he lay on his back in utter darkness, puzzling about the events of the evening. He and some of the other men had searched the slope by lantern light. They had found only a few scattered hoof-marks at its top, and these pointed every which way. There was no hope of tracking the killer in the dark, and they might as well not have tried. Whoever he was, he seemed to have planned carefully and to have patiently waited his chance. And he seemed to be familiar with this station and the country around it.

"Did you find anything?" Susan said.

"Nothing. I thought you were asleep."

"Alone in a room where a man was killed? Hardly."

"You could have moved in with that other woman passenger. Under the circumstances, I'm surprised she didn't ask you to."

"She's a hardy pioneer type. Besides, I like the idea of having you nearby. That's what I'm paying you for, isn't it?"

"I wouldn't know."

"What do you mean by that?"

"I'm wondering what this has to do with you."

After a pause, Susan said, "Or what I have to do with murder?"

"I didn't say that."

"But you were thinking it."

"No." His eyes were getting accustomed to the darkness and he could make out the dim pattern of massive rafters above him. He could hear Susan moving in the bed. He turned and saw that she was sitting up, hugging her knees. "I was thinking that it's strange that the killer knew Nooner would be in here and was watching this window."

"Yes." The thought seemed to have occurred to Susan, too. "Could one of the other passengers have done it?"

"The Mormon, the woman, and one of the stationkeepers were together in the dining room when they heard the shot and your scream. I don't know where Ramirez was."

"Could he have done it?"

"Doesn't seem likely. Where would he get a rifle? And it looked like the killer had a horse waiting at the top of the slope."

"Could Wiggins have got this far?" Susan said. "We passed him a little after noon."

"He could have made it by trading horses two or three

times at stage stations or ranches. Would he have a reason to kill Nooner?"

"I certainly don't know of any. Of course, they were both in Star City in the old days. And Wiggins seems to have gone back there from time to time. There might have been something between them, I suppose."

The pattern of the rafters was more distant now. A frail cord of moonlight linked a flaw in the roof with the foot of Susan's bed. A breeze jostled the locked shutter.

"I hate this," Susan said. "All of it. The money isn't worth it . . . it's funny. There's a part of me that doesn't want the money, that can never want it. Can you understand that?"

"You must have known it might be messy," Steve said.

"No. I thought it would be simple and easy. Steve, I can't believe that Mr. Nooner's death has anything to do with the treasure. He must have had enemies . . ."

"Think carefully, Susan. Do you know of anyone else who might be in this?"

"No, Steve. No one."

"No one could have been following you?"

"No. I'm certain."

"What about your husband?"

"He— No one followed me from Iowa, Steve. How could they? The next train would get them to Ogden twenty-four hours behind me. They couldn't possibly be here tonight."

Steve stretched and yawned and tried to sound casual. "Tell me about your husband, Susan. Your present one."

"I should think you'd be more interested in Ben Roman."

"All right, then. Ben Roman."

She sighed noisily and sank back into the bed. "He was a most likable person, always laughing and doing little kindnesses. I went to Star City to be with a married sister, who was going to have a baby. I was seventeen. I met Ben in November and we were married on Christmas Day. He was a mining-district judge. He was trusted and respected by everyone.

"The passes filled with snow that winter, and Star City was isolated for two months. There was very little food and no medicine. My sister's baby died when it was a few days old. There was a thaw in February, and she and her husband made arrangements to leave on the first stage out. Ben insisted that I go with them. He promised to join me in a few weeks.

"There was no railroad then, and we were delayed in Salt Lake City for two weeks, waiting to get an eastbound stage. While we were there, the news came that the vigilantes had hanged Ben. He had confessed before he died. He had been at the head of more than a hundred thieves and killers. The newspapers called his organization the most ruthless gang of criminals this country has ever seen."

The last words were almost inaudible. Now there was a stillness in which the air seemed brittle.

"Your family and friends back in Iowa never learned that you were married to him?" Steve said.

"The letter telling my parents of the marriage had been held up by the snows. It had gone out on the same stage I had taken and it arrived in Cedar Rapids at the same time. I managed to get it before it reached my parents."

"And Wiggins? Where does he fit in?"

"He was a neighbor from Iowa who happened to be in Star City at the time of my marriage. After I went home, I heard nothing of him for years—I think he was in jail for a time—and I practically forgot about him. Then he turned up. He had been back to Star City and had heard rumors of Ben Roman's buried treasure. He got friendly with my sister and my brother-in-law. They let it slip that Ben had once mentioned hidden money to me.

"I had done everything I could to put my few months in Star City out of my mind. I had told myself that when Ben confessed, he must have told the vigilantes where the money was hidden. Wiggins was sure that he had not.

"Well, Wiggins wanted me to go back with him, get the money, and share it with him. He begged and promised and threatened. I stalled—I couldn't refuse him outright because of all he knew about me.

"My parents died and then, last fall, my brother-in-law was killed in a runaway. He left nothing but debts, and we needed money desperately, and I decided to come back. I meant to make the trip and get money without Wiggins' knowing, as I told you. But there he was in Ogden."

She concluded wearily, and for a time neither spoke. A breeze seeped through cracks in the log building and touched Steve's face deliciously.

"I'm still curious about your present husband," he said cautiously.

"Altogether too curious."

"What was he doing while Wiggins was plaguing you?"

"Nothing that concerns us now." Impatience colored her voice.

"I have a feeling he didn't know about Wiggins."

"Have all the feelings you want."

"You don't like to talk about him," Steve persisted. "Why not?"

"All right! He's four feet tall and cross-eyed. He has a naked woman tattooed in the middle of his forehead and when he frowns, she dances. He chews garlic and he beats me after every meal."

"I'll be damned," Steve said. "I'd like to meet him."

That ended the talk, and after a while he drifted into sleep. His last conscious thought was that for the first day in months he hadn't had a pack of cards in his hands. Still he dreamed of the Game, dreamed he was holding a four-flush and an ace that kept changing from one suit to another.

He woke cold and unable to get comfortable. He could hear Susan's even breathing from the far side of the bed. Picking up his blankets, he quietly crossed the room. Very gently, he lay down beside her, pulling his own blankets over him.

The scraping and banging of the rickety door woke him, and he sat up. Susan had come into the room, fully dressed even to her tiny hat with the veil laid back across it. It was broad daylight, and Steve looked around the room in bewilderment. He was not usually a heavy sleeper.

"They're getting ready to bury Mr. Nooner," Susan said. "Then we're going to have breakfast and be on our way. One of the station men will drive."

Steve threw off the blankets and swung his feet to the floor.

"I'll get out of here while you wash," Susan said. At the door, she stopped and said, "You know what you are? You're a liar. You snored all night."

# FIVE

Twilight lay amber on Star City as Tim Gaul bore across Center Street, bending from the waist in the driving, heavy-shouldered walk that made him recognizable half a mile away. The stage was late, and a knot of men waited under the hotel arcade. Tim nodded to those who greeted him. He took a place off to himself where he could view the length of the street. Outwardly, he waited calmly, his leonine features impassive. Inwardly, he struggled agonizingly. For Tim Gaul knew that he was losing his mind.

This morning, for instance, he had got out of bed thinking he was to lead the vigilantes on a scout. He had loaded his shotgun with a dozen revolver balls and had started to put on his buffalo coat. It was only when he saw the Blacktail buttes free of snow and realized that the season was summer that he began to understand that the days of scouts and hangings were somewhere in the past.

He had captained the dismal winter marches into the

wilderness, had sat as judge when the quarry was captured, and he had acted as hangman some two dozen times. His mind had seized on the grim excitement, it seemed, and now refused to let go of it. It was as if past and present had reversed themselves. The events of today seemed to occur already half-forgotten; those of that long-ago winter were vivid and immediate.

Even as the stage swung out of the gulch into the lower end of Center Street, Tim fought the past out of his mind and tried to remember why he had come here. It had nothing to do with the Roman gang, he told himself. The really bad ones were dead and the others had got out of the territory. Luke Lumby was the only really bad one who had escaped—with the gang's treasure, according to Ben Roman's gallows confession. Did meeting the stage have something to do with Luke Lumby? No, no. This was 1874, according to the calendar Jase Nooner had given Tim. Where had all those years gone? Jase said— Jase Nooner, that was it! Jase would be driving the stage. He would take Tim home with him for a decent meal, and afterward they would talk.

But it wasn't Jase Nooner who wrapped the reins around the brake handle and climbed down from the driver's seat when the coach had pulled up. It was a man Tim didn't think he knew.

Sheriff Bill Illingsley pushed through the crowd and peered over his spectacles at the stranger. A good man, the sheriff. He had the looks and manner of a slow-witted schoolteacher, but Tim knew that under the surface he was a flint-hard lawman who gave the town the harsh regulation it needed. Now, in his maddeningly deliberate way, he got around to asking the question that was in Tim's mind.

43

"Where's the regular driver?"

"Dead. Shot in the back. Happened in my station a day out of Ogden."

"The stage was robbed?" Illingsley asked.

The driver shook his head. "Looked like a grudge killing to me. Nooner stood in front of a window. Somebody was laying out in the brush and got him from ambush. We buried him. Couldn't track the killer."

"I'll want the exact of it," the sheriff said. "In my office. Soon as you're unloaded."

Jase Nooner dead! Struggling with this realization, Tim released his slippery hold on time altogether. Past and present were no longer two conflicting concepts that he had to choose between; they became one. The Roman gang had got old Jase; they were making a last stand. As long as one of them remained alive, honest folks weren't safe.

Tim studied the passengers as they climbed out of the coach. The small, dark-haired man in the gray riding coat was worth a second look. But it was the big, scar-faced fellow who caught Tim's interest and stirred suspicion in him. Good man or bad, he was a hard case . . . He had a woman with him, it seemed—a trim, young-breasted little fixin' whose face was hidden by a veil.

Tim followed them into the hotel. While the man signed the register, the woman stood at the foot of the stairs and idly scanned the faded elegance of the lobby. Tim gave her his back and strode through the doorway of the adjoining bar, turning guardedly for another look.

The big man joined her, and as they started up the staircase, she threw back her veil. The glimpse that Tim Gaul had of her face staggered him like a blow. Hardly knowing what he was doing, he followed to the bottom of the steps and stared after the couple. When they reached the landing and rounded a turn, he saw her face again. And all doubt left him.

He wheeled toward the desk and collided with the young man in the long gray coat, who was headed toward the stairway. Tim's irritation turned to surprise as the man apologized in Spanish.

*"Mil pardones, señor."*

Tim grunted and pushed on to the desk, where he eyed the clerk defiantly and spun the register around. Above the Mexican's ornate signature he made out *Major & Mrs. S. Tanager, Denver*.

So Mrs. Ben Roman had a new name, he thought, and she had the nerve to come back. There were folks in town who stood up for her on occasion, saying that she had no knowledge of Ben Roman's real nature; but Tim had no patience with this view. A criminal's wife was a criminal, he always asserted, wagging his head as if quoting some ancient and unquestionable axiom.

He returned to the street, where the Gilmer and Salisbury stableman was climbing onto the stage to take it to the barn. The sheriff and the driver were headed up the walk toward the courthouse. Tim lunged into a heavy-footed lope and caught them.

"Bill!" he bellowed. "That was Sue Roman on that stage. She's at the hotel with a new husband!"

Bill Illingsley turned and stared thoughtfully at the planks in the sidewalk. His first reaction was that this was another of Tim's addled notions. Still, you never could tell about Tim; every once in a while he came up with useful information. Besides, having ridden with the vigilantes, Bill respected Tim for the tough-minded leader he had once been. The old boy was at least entitled to a courteous reply. Bill took a moment to phrase one properly.

"That so?" he said.

"You're jumping damn right it's so!"

"Well now," Bill studied the fading rose sky above the Blacktails. "It's been a considerable spell since you put eyes on her, Tim."

"Have a look for your own damn self," Tim said impatiently.

"Can't say as I remember her too well, excepting she was a bell-ringer for pretty. Besides, it seems to me the women on that stage were wearing veils."

Tim understood that he wasn't being taken seriously. This made him furious.

"She lifted her veil when she went up the stairs, you turtle-headed idiot! There's something going on, and you better wake up to it!"

"You betcha, Tim," Bill said. Tim wasn't always so sure of himself, he thought. Either the old boy was getting worse or he had really seen something. "I'll go around and have a look at her. Right off, I got to question this man about Jase."

Tim watched the two men amble on up the street to the courthouse. He muttered to himself, foully, cursing whatever it was that happened to a man that made folks doubt him. He cast a look over the town, which was taking on a weird unreality in the thinning light, and he fought off wild impulses that tore at him. He struggled with time again now, not facing the issue squarely but knowing a gnawing doubt of his ability to think straight. Yet this was hardly a matter of thought, he decided. A man could believe his eyes. As if in answer to his tugging restlessness, light bloomed in a window across the street. It was the window of Anne Barabee's dressmaking shop, and after a moment of blinking indecision, Tim headed for it.

He couldn't rightly approve of Anne, for she had been an outlaw's girl; yet he didn't condemn her as glibly as he did Sue Roman. In the little contact he had had with Anne, she had always been friendly and respectful. And she had paid for her mistake—well, at least partly.

She had been a gay thing, too gay. Half the young men in the territory had run after her. When she had taken up with Luke Lumby, even her own folks had turned against her. Luke had left her alone and mighty near friendless. Folks had said she would take to a hurdy-gurdy house, or to something worse, but she hadn't. She made her living by dressmaking—and a scant living it was, the way Tim heard it. Though she was not yet thirty, she was spoken of as an old maid.

He found her standing at a table, cutting a dress out of some silky blue material. She was surprised to have him drop in, but she smiled courteously and asked if he would like to sit down. He shook his head.

"Sue Roman is in town," he said.

Anne's scissors clattered on the table. After one gaping instant, she regained her composure and smiled again.

"That can't be so, Captain Gaul."

"Saw her plain as I see you. Sheriff don't believe me."

"That's too bad," Anne said cautiously, using the same tone she would use to a child. She was a little frightened, not of Tim but of his crazy ideas.

"She came on the stage. Chances are she'll head for the dining room right off. You could have a look for yourself and tell the sheriff it's her. I'd be obliged."

"Tell you what—" Anne picked up the scissors and studied the pattern she had laid out of the material. "I have work to do. I'll see her tomorrow."

47

Tim watched her work, his face immobile. After a long moment, he wheeled abruptly and went into the street.

Anne sank into a chair, clutching the scissors like a weapon. Captain Gaul was getting worse, she thought. He had lived in the past for a long time; now he was seeing faces out of the past. He would be seeing Luke's face next. Something should be done about him.

But was there any chance he had really seen Sue? Could she have come back for the treasure after all these years?

In a few minutes Tim Gaul pushed into the room again. His eagerness was almost pathetic.

"She's in the dining room. You can get a look at her from the street."

Anne snatched a shawl from a peg and arranged it over her dark blond, gray-threaded hair. She gave him a curt little nod and followed him out.

Darkness drenched the street now. Lighted windows laid frail and ghostly patterns across the boardwalks. The doorway of a saloon was a garish tunnel in the night; inside, a piano tinkled dutifully. Anne strained to keep up as Tim angled across the street toward the faded rose curtains of the hotel dining room. He reached them first and stepped aside, pointing.

The room was crowded, but Anne picked her out at once. She was sitting at a table with a wide-shouldered man whose back was toward the window. She was smiling at something he had said. Anne gasped. This was unquestionably Sue Roman—but not the shy, too-eager seventeen-year-old whom Anne remembered. Here was a woman of poise and grace that were discernible at a glance.

"She's lovely!" Anne whispered.

"Told you it's her," Tim said. "Now you get down to the courthouse and tell Bill Illingsley."

Thoughts were racing winds that tore and tumbled through Anne's being. The only decision she could make was to be cautious.

"She does resemble Sue," she said.

Tim cussed unabashedly. "It's her!"

"I wouldn't want to swear to it, Captain Gaul. Tell you what—let's not make a fuss about this. Wouldn't it be smarter to just sort of watch and wait?"

Sue had come back for the treasure. That was a certainty, Anne thought. For Anne knew what others might only guess at: Ben Roman had lied when he said that Luke Lumby had got away with the gang's loot. On that bleak and death-cold afternoon when Luke had left the country, he was broke. He had borrowed Anne's last twenty dollars for supplies.

Tim was regarding her woodenly, his face strangely animal-like in the hazy light from the window. Anne forced herself to smile and to touch his arm.

"I've got to get back to work, Captain Gaul. Remember, no fuss."

She headed toward the light of her shop, clutching at her shawl and lifting her skirt above the dust of the street. Behind her, Tim whined his protest to the night.

"They're comin' back! They killed Jase Nooner and they're comin' back!"

# SIX

Five days on that stage, Steve thought. Five days away from the Game. And the clink of chips in the hotel barroom had stirred no tantalizing urge in him.

He lay on his bed with his boots off and studied his toes. He could hear Susan in the next room, scuffing around in bedroom slippers. There was a sort of solace in this sound of her nearness, and there was a challenge in it, too.

She seemed confident that she knew where the money was and that there was a large amount. He was not a man to concern himself with ethical niceties; but as far as he could see, she had no better claim to it than anybody else. It would belong to whoever got possession of it and got it out of the territory . . .

The door that joined their rooms swung open, and Susan came in. She was wearing a kimono, and her hair was fastened in a ridiculous knot on top of her head. It pleased him that she hadn't knocked.

"There's someone at my door," she said. "You answer. I'll sneak through your room and down the hall to the bathroom.''

He swung off the bed, caught her by the shoulders, and held her at arm's length. There was surprise in her eyes, and a glint of apprehension, too.

"You've got ears," he said. "I never saw them before.''

She feigned exasperation and, smiling faintly, backed out of his grip. "You get in there and answer my door.''

He let his hands slap his sides and obeyed, closing the connecting door behind him. He opened the door on a tall, long-necked man who peered at him over lopsided spectacles.

"Come in, Sheriff. I wondered if you'd be along.''

Bill Illingsley stepped into the room, took a moment to look it over, cleared his throat.

"I'm told you and your wife were present when Jase Nooner was murdered," he said.

"We were.'' Steve lifted Susan's skirt from a chair and laid it on the bed. "Sit down.''

The sheriff laid hold of the back of the chair but didn't sit. He gave the room another looking over, seeming to take a special interest in the upper corners of it.

"I want the exact of it, Major Tanager.''

"There was no rhyme or reason to it," Steve said. "The man came to our room. He stood in front of an open window, and somebody got him. He was dead when he hit the floor.''

"Just you and your wife there?''

"Yes.''

"Why did Jase come to your room?''

"No special reason," Steve said.

The sheriff stared down at his boots. He seemed embarrassed. Steve guessed that the stationkeeper had told him of the conversation at supper that night.

"Nooner and my wife were trying to remember where they had seen each other before. They were making a sort of joke out of it."

"That so?" the sheriff said.

Steve nodded politely. There was a pause. The sheriff cleared his throat.

"Could I have a word with your wife?"

"She's taking a bath."

The sheriff changed his mind and sat down in the chair. It took him a moment to get his legs crossed and his holstered revolver adjusted.

"I'll ask you straight out," he said. "Did you shoot Jase?"

"Damn damnation! Why would I shoot him?"

"Something to do with your wife?"

"You know damn well I didn't shoot him," Steve said. "That bullet came from outside. We went out with a lantern and found sign at the top of the slope. Those are things the station man and the other passengers will confirm."

The sheriff nodded slowly, seeming to accept this. But the little blue eyes that peeped over the low-riding spectacles were hard and cold as stone. Steve saw that under the maddening slow-minded manner of this man there was a core of spring steel.

"What's your business in Star City, Major?"

"I came to look over some property."

"What property?"

"That's confidential."

"Representing somebody else?"

"You might say so," Steve said.

The sheriff tilted back in his chair. "Sit down, Major. I dislike talking to a man towering over me like a tree in the wind."

Steve swallowed a blunt reply. He arranged the pillows on Susan's bed for a back rest and swung his stockinged feet off the floor.

"There are things a stranger ought to know about Star City," the sheriff said.

"I'd be pleased to know them."

"In the boom days isolation and gold made this town a mighty attractive place for criminals. We got 'em by the herd, and they organized. One murder per day, average. Sluggings, sluice robberies, holdups by the hundreds. The vigilantes struck like Death itself. When the cleanup was over, they set up county law, courts, peace officers.

"But the wild days left a wound that didn't heal, Major. The citizens are ashamed of those days and scared they'll come back. They insist on the tightest kind of regulation. I give it to 'em. Gambling, saloons, hurdy-gurdy halls—all operate orderly. A man gets one drink too much, I jail him. He packs a gun, I do the same. Card sharks get special handling. I usually just pass the word around when I see one cheating. Last one we had got nailed to a door by his hands."

"I get it," Steve said. "You think I might be a card shark."

"Thought crossed my mind."

Steve wondered if the man was deliberately trying to goad him into anger. The sheriff got slowly and awkwardly to his feet.

"Got to get along," he said. "Sorry I missed your wife."

"Good night," Steve said. He didn't move from the

bed until after the sheriff had gone. Then he got up and turned the key in the lock. He went back to his own room and lighted a cigar, congratulating himself on controlling his temper.

In a few minutes Susan came back, her head turbaned in a towel.

"The sheriff paid us a call," Steve said.

"I know. He was waiting in the hall. He stared at me and blinked and adjusted his glasses and stared again. I don't know if he recognized me or not."

"Should he have?"

"I danced with him once. I remember because he was so utterly awkward."

"If he recognized you in that getup, he's pretty good," Steve said.

She cocked her chin at him in the teasingly defiant way she had, and she passed close to him as she crossed toward the connecting door. The fresh, faintly soapy smell of her touched his nostrils, and he was aware of the satin litheness of her body within the sheath of the kimono.

"Susan—"

She pushed quickly into her room and turned the key behind her. He stepped to the door and knocked on it.

"That won't do," he said. "I'm your bodyguard. I don't want a locked door between us."

"That's pretty silly," she called.

After a moment, she unlocked the door and poked her head into his room. She was very serious. "All right. It will stay unlocked, provided that is nowise taken as an invitation."

"Nowise," he said.

She closed the door at once. He went down to the lobby to order more hot water, then to the bathroom for his own bath. When he returned to his room, he went to the connecting door and tried it. He opened it just a crack at first, then pulled it wider. She was kneeling beside the bed, head bowed, her lips moving.

He quietly pushed the door shut and retreated. The simple thing he had seen had shaken him. He gripped the footboard of his bed and waited out the surge of emotion as he might a wave of pain.

*You can't have her, and if you could, you'd destroy her*, he thought. *Quite possibly you'll destroy her anyhow. So the hell with her. Think about the money; that's what's important. A princess at her prayers, and the hell with her . . .*

Steve ate his breakfast in the hotel dining room, then carried Susan's up to her on a tray. Following her instructions, he walked to the livery at the end of the street, rented a horse and buggy, and drove it to the hotel. She came out immediately, wearing a veil.

She gave the directions, and they drove back and forth through the town, not missing a street. She pointed out the house where she had lived as Ben Roman's bride, and other houses that she knew. Next, they drove up Star Gulch, following a narrow road with the hillsides above them pockmarked with mineshafts, most of them abandoned. When they had gone about a mile, they came to a place to turn around and went back, passing the town and taking the stage road down-gulch. He understood, of course, that the purpose of all this driving was to conceal Susan's real object. Whatever it was that she wanted to see, she was determined to attract no special attention to it.

Star Gulch was a long, creek-threaded crease in the earth shaped like a bow. At the center of its curve, two side gulches joined it from the east. In one of these and on the

55

slopes above it, the weathered buildings of the town lay in a ragged shotgun pattern. Across the creek and a bit down-gulch, two wedge-shaped, relatively level areas were separated by a steep spur. These and the side gulches formed the star that gave the main gulch, the creek, and the town their names.

The upper of the flats was barren except for a single shack and a short length of sluice. Two Chinese, naked to the waist, queues wagging across their backs, were shoveling gravel into the sluice. Susan gave them hardly a glance. She kept looking back along the road, frowning.

"I think we're being followed," she said finally.

"The man on the mule?" Steve said. "He's been with us all morning."

The lower flat was a triangular area of maybe eighty acres, stabbing into the surrounding hills as if it had been scooped out by a gigantic arrowhead. Its lower end was cluttered with sheds and cabins, netted with sluice, and teeming with laboring Chinese. Susan directed Steve to cross the creek by a log bridge, and they entered the area.

"This is Union Flat," she said. "It was once considered the most promising placer ground in the gulch."

"It always happens," Steve said. "The high pay peters out, and the glory-roaders move on. The Chinese come in and work the tailings. It's said they can live on twenty-five cents a day."

"And if they should accidentally hit a rich lode, the good Caucasians will find some righteous reason for driving them out," Susan said sarcastically. As if surprised at herself, she quickly added, "I suppose that's awfully hypocritical, coming from a criminal's wife."

"Let that wound heal," he said gently.

"I thought it had. Coming here has opened it."

They drove a twisting course among shacks, mounds of tailings, knots of workmen who shoveled or panned or shook rockers and scarcely gave the buggy a glance. As they rolled on up the flat, the buildings and the activity thinned out, then disappeared.

"Pull up," Susan said.

From here to the upper point of its triangle, the sage-studded flat was empty except for two log cabins, bleached almost white by sun and moisture. To the south, a mine entrance made a neat black square in the wall of the spur.

"This end never produced much gold," Susan said chattily.

"Oh?" Steve said. He had a hunch that they weren't too far from the treasure. He tried not to let her see how closely he was watching her, waiting for the anxious look, the second glance that would point to the hiding place.

"Ben had an interest in a claim around here some-where."

"Oh?" he said again. "He had some legitimate interests then?"

Susan gave him an inquiring glance and seemed to realize that he hadn't meant to be sarcastic. "Ben had a talent for business. He had terrific energy, and a way with people. But thinking back, I believe he must have had some sort of compulsion to deceive. I remember little things, lies he told when the truth would have been easier, things like that . . ."

She scanned the flat as she spoke, not centering her attention anywhere in particular. When she leaned out of the buggy to glance behind them, he looked back, too. The man on the mule had stopped some fifty yards away.

"Who do you suppose he is?" Susan said.

"We can turn back and ask him."

"Let's pretend not to notice him. Circle back to the road."

They followed the stage road down-gulch another mile, swinging close to the great black butte that marked the north end of the Blacktails. Finally, they took a side road that meandered over rolling country and finally brought them back into town from the northeast.

Steve dropped Susan at the hotel before returning the buggy to the livery. As he left the barn, he saw the man on the mule jog up to the hotel, dismount, and go in. He was a stocky man in a beaded elkskin vest and a low-crowned, broad-brimmed hat.

Steve quickened his step. Entering the lobby, he saw the man at the bar, posted where he could watch the stairs through the connecting doorway. Steve went in and took a place beside him.

A grin creased the man's round face. He was younger than Steve had thought at first. He was drinking buttermilk, and he raised his glass in salutation. Steve caught a glimpse of a badge under the beaded vest.

*"Name is Birk. Mostly I'm called Smiley."*

"Tanager," Steve said.

"I know that well enough." Birk sipped the buttermilk and smacked his lips. "Guess you know I been tailin' you all morning."

Steve extended a finger and pushed back the edge of the beaded vest to expose the badge. "Line of duty?"

Smiley Birk grinned again. "It's what the sheriff wants. What were you looking for down on Fan-tan Flat?"

"Fan-tan Flat?"

"Where you stopped for a look around."

58

"Susan called it Union Flat."

"Used to be. Name changed when the coolies moved in. Mind telling me why you went down there?"

"No reason," Steve said. "Just looking over the country."

"Likely enough, far as I'm concerned. Sheriff won't believe it, though."

The bartender edged toward them, and Steve ordered buttermilk. He said, "Suspicious man, the sheriff."

"Don't often set a full-time watch on strangers, though. You're getting special treatment."

"Waste of tax money."

Birk pushed his hat to the back of his head and rested his elbows on the bar. "Hell, we got six deputies. In this town, Mister, you look four ways before you spit." Birk caught Steve's eye and jerked his head significantly toward the lobby. " 'Course, it ain't only the law that's keeping tabs on you."

Steve turned. A rough-hewn, pale-eyed man loitered just beyond the doorway. Birk watched Steve's face closely.

"Tim Gaul," Birk said.

"I've heard of him—'Tim Gaul, the Angel of Wrath.' "

"Tim is near the end of the road Wit-scrambled, you might say. Comes of strangling too many and liking it too well."

Steve drank deeply of the buttermilk, finding it thick and cool. "And you think he's watching me?"

Birk nodded, grinning. "Part of my job is to keep an eye on *him*. Can't tell what cockeyed notion he might take."

"He was following us, too?"

"In a way of speaking. What he did, he climbed up to his cabin atop Sunrise Ridge, just east of town. He can see the whole town from up there and most of the gulch. They say he keeps a spyglass up there."

Steve drained his glass and put it down. He produced two cigars, one of which he gave to Birk. "I'll be seeing you."

"Can't help yourself," Birk grinned.

Tim Gaul had taken a chair that gave him a view into the bar. Steve stopped in front of him and held out his hand. Tim glared suspiciously.

"I'd like to shake the hand of the famous Tim Gaul," Steve said.

Tim hesitated, then pulled himself to his feet. His handclasp was weak. As he sank back into his chair, he muttered something that sounded like "Thank you kindly."

"I'd like to talk to you about the vigilantes," Steve said. "I'd like a firsthand account."

Tim studied him closely. He shook his head to the cigar Steve offered. Then the tension seemed to go out of him and he nodded curtly.

"Pull up that chair there," he said.

As Steve did this, Carlos Ramirez left his seat a few yards away and moved to a closer one.

# SEVEN

When Susan reached her room, the door across the hall was open. She glimpsed a slender, roughly dressed man kneeling to unfasten the straps of a blanket roll. He was having an awkward time of it because he wore a pistol in a long holster that was tied to his right leg. Another man, whom she couldn't see, was swearing about something. As she inserted her key in her lock, she heard the first man shush the other. Their door closed gently as she swung open her own.

Something about the incident disturbed her, but she immediately chided herself. What could be less suspicious than two men getting settled in a hotel room? Being followed by that man on the mule had made her jumpy, she supposed. It was going to be very difficult to get the treasure if her every move was to be watched.

It had been a relief to see the cabin squatting there on the desolate end of the flat much as she remembered it. At the same time, its weathered appearance had startled her, for she remembered it as a raw new building. Now impatience stabbed at her. The treasure was there for the taking, yet there must be days of delay before she could take it.

In all probability, the cabin was occupied—very likely by Chinese. She would have to find out who owned the property now. It would have to be bought without attracting attention. She would have to move in very quietly and quickly, take the treasure, and leave the territory. She and Steve. And Wiggins. Wiggins would be very much in on it.

On the whole, she was thankful for that wild impulse back in Ogden that had led to her hiring Steve, although there was much about him that disturbed her. He was strong and quiet and capable. He was very pleasant company. He had the manners of a gentleman. He was considerate of her. That was really all she knew about him in a matter-of-fact, sensible way. But there was more, so much more that she couldn't put into words. The scarred face. The too-rare smile that made him seem almost boyish. The sharply tragic spectacle of a gentleman's effort to cheat at cards. These things moved her and frightened her. And they made her wonder if she was a fool to trust him at all.

She had taken off her hat and veil and was straightening her hair when the timid knock came. She opened the door on a slender woman with graying blond hair. Susan regarded her inquisitively, then she caught her breath.

"Why—Anne! Anne Barabee!"

"Hello, Sue." Anne smiled uncertainly.

"Well, come in!" Susan said. "Good heavens! I didn't imagine you'd still be in town. I mean—"

"I didn't know if you would want to see me."

"It's wonderful to see you."

"I saw you in the dining room last night," Anne said. "Tim Gaul recognized you, too. But I've said nothing to anyone. And Tim—" She explained that Tim was a little mixed up in the head and that folks weren't likely to pay much attention to him.

"I'm afraid the sheriff is on to me, too," Susan said. "At least, he's suspicious."

Susan stood with her back to the door. For a moment, there seemed to be nothing more to say, then the women suddenly embraced.

They had never been close in the old days. Anne was older, and she had made herself an object of criticism by taking up with Luke Lumby, whom the whole town hated and feared. Susan had criticized along with everyone else—never dreaming that she had married Luke's boss. Now they were two of a kind, she and Anne, and they were drawn together.

"The past dies hard in Star City," Anne said, as if reading Susan's thoughts.

They sat down and exchanged smiles. Susan said, "Tell me about yourself."

"I'm an old maid," Anne said cheerfully.

"Why, Anne, that's ridiculous. You're lovely and the term doesn't fit at all. There are plenty of—"

"Stop it," Anne said. "The only men who come near me have the idea I'm an easy mark because I was Luke Lumby's girl."

"I'm surprised you've stayed here then."

"I thought I could live down a foolish mistake." Anne had a pleasant way of smiling while she spoke. "I'm still trying."

They chatted about other things then, the town and its people and the changes that eight years had brought.

Suddenly Anne said, "You've come back for the treasure, haven't you?"

Susan was caught off guard. "What on earth do you mean?"

"Luke told me that Ben Roman had a big cache of money somewhere. Why else would you come back? . . . Don't look so upset, Sue. I merely want to help if I can."

"I suppose there would be rumors about a treasure," Susan said vaguely.

"I'm not trying to get my finger in the pie," Anne said. "I didn't mean that."

Anne seemed perfectly sincere. In any case, Susan thought, it would be nice to have a woman to chat with from time to time. When Anne got up to leave, Susan said, "Will you join us for dinner tonight? We're planning to have it brought here to my room."

"I'd love to," Anne said.

A few minutes after she had left, Steve appeared. He had coffee and sandwiches on a tray.

"We missed lunch," he said.

Susan accepted a cup of coffee. Steve bit into a sandwich voraciously.

"Wiggins is here," he said.

"Already?"

"I saw his name in the register. He must've just arrived."

Watching Steve devour the sandwiches gave Susan an appetite and she tried one. She told of Anne's visit, and he explained that he had been getting acquainted with the deputy who had followed them, and with Tim Gaul.

"You do have a way of taking the bull by the horns," she said.

They had scarcely finished the coffee when Wiggins knocked on the door. He wore the same checked suit, rumpled and stained beyond belief now. He pushed into the room in an effluvium of stale sweat, horse and human.

"I hope no one saw you come here," Susan said.

Wiggins chuckled. "Nobody sees what Slim Wiggins don't want seen."

"What room are you in?" Steve demanded.

"Thirty-six. Next floor up."

Steve held out his hand. "Give me your key I want a look at your gear. Hand it over."

"Now you look ahere, Major—"

Steve seized him by the collar with both hands and slammed him into a chair with a shock that threatened to shatter it.

"Steve!" Susan said. "There's no point in acting like—like a tyrant."

"I want his key and I'm going to get it. Maybe you'd better go in the other room."

He plunged a hand under the left side of Wiggin's coat and came up with a revolver. Frightened now, Wiggins produced the key. Shoving the gun under his belt, Steve slammed out of the room. Susan and Wiggins exchanged frowns.

"That there man is out of his head," Wiggins said.

"I never know what he's going to do," Susan conceded wearily.

She crossed the room to the small table that served as a desk. Dipping a pen into the inkpot, she quickly made marks on a sheet of writing paper. Wiggins got up to look over her shoulder.

"This is a map," she said, pushing the paper into his hands. "It shows the property I want."

65

Wiggins stared eagerly as her slender finger pointed to the symbols she had made.

"That's the old mine in the spur south of Union Flat. These are the cabins. Lots were staked out down there in the old days. This cabin and the lot it's on is what we want."

"The money is in the cabin?"

"I'm not going to tell you exactly where it is. You're to go to the courthouse and find out who owns this property now. It used to belong to one of Ben's business partners—Abner Gill. Maybe he still owns it. Maybe it's been abandoned and you can get title to it by paying back taxes or something."

"Like as not, the bank has taken the place over," Wiggins said. "Anyhow, it shouldn't cost much."

"After you get it, you can clear the Chinese out—quietly. Then you'll deed the property to me. I want title to it if we can possibly get it—even if that means delay."

Steve pushed into the room, carrying a Winchester rifle he had brought from Wiggins' room. He waved it under Wiggins' nose.

"Brand new," he said. "You left Ogden in the middle of the night. You must have bought this in Brigham City."

"I did," Wiggins said. "Man don't like to ride through the wilderness without he has a good rifle."

"You listen to me. You are not to carry any kind of weapon as long as we're here. If you do, I'll take it as a personal affront."

"Major, a man has got a right—"

*"Do you understand that—"* The words were as incisive as a razor slash. "Maybe I can make it plainer. If you ever come armed into my presence, I'll kill you where you stand."

Wiggins grinned helplessly, nodded slightly, and turned away.

"Steve!" Susan said. "After all, we have to work together."

"That's right, Major." Wiggins managed to look genuinely hurt. "I'm only trying to work together with you people."

"And you're going to do it without weapons. I'll return your guns when we leave here."

"Let's go over what you're to do," Susan said to Wiggins. "Then you can get out of here and get busy."

Steve listened moodily while she and Wiggins reviewed her plan. He took the map from Wiggins and studied it with a frown, annoyed that Susan hadn't seen fit to tell him about the cabin. He said nothing until Wiggins was on his way to the door. Then he tapped the man's chest with a finger.

"One mistake and you're through. Do you understand that?"

Wiggins flashed his yellow grin. "There'll be no mistakes if we all work together with each other."

When he had left the room, Susan sighed heavily. "Steve, is it wise to be so rough with him?"

"The first time I ever saw you, you aimed a hatpin at his middle."

"I detest him. But what can you gain by bullying him?"

"I'll stay alive, maybe. Anyway, two approaches are better than one—I'll bully, you pacify."

Susan considered this soberly. "I had come to think of you as a very direct man. Now I'm wondering if you aren't devious, after all."

"Just hope I'm devious enough to deal with that weasel."

Steve spent the rest of the afternoon walking around town, visiting a barber shop, buying some shirts. Several times he was aware of Smiley Birk watching from a distance.

He had a before-dinner whiskey in the hotel bar and got up to their rooms at exactly six-thirty. He knew that Susan had asked Anne to come at that time and he expected to find the two women chatting, but Susan was alone. When a waitress brought the dinner a few minutes later, Anne still hadn't arrived. Finally, they ate without her.

Anne Barabee seldom went anywhere except to Sunday service, and she was very much looking forward to having a meal with Susan and her husband. She had intended to stop work early and primp a bit; but as luck would have it, one of her customers was late for a fitting, and it was well after six before Anne was free.

She swiftly tidied the shop and hurried into the small back room in which she cooked, ate, and slept. She poured cold water into a basin and washed her face. She would redo her hair, she decided, and be off. She was drying her face on a flour-sack towel when she heard someone enter the shop.

She called, but got no answer. Then the curtain on the doorway between this room and the shop was jerked aside, and two men confronted her.

"We mean you no harm, Miss Barabee," one said quickly.

He was young and rather good-looking. The other was of the same slender build, but older. He seemed to have a bunch of feathers growing out of his right shoulder; on second glance, Anne saw that this was the feathered handle of a throwing knife. It was held by a sheath sewed to his leather vest. He drew a folded paper from his pocket and handed it to her.

"Friend of ours wants to see you," the first man said.

"We got horses in the alley," the feathered man said. "Sidesaddle for you, ma'am."

"Anyone who wants to see me can come here," Anne said. She added haughtily, "And knock properly."

She unfolded the paper and turned it so the light from a window fell on it. She read the scrawled words hurriedly and then slowly. For a moment she was unable to speak.

"How about it?" the younger man said.

"Yes," Anne said in a small voice. "Yes, I'll go with you. Is it far?"

"A short ride and a hard climb," the feathered man said.

She should have guessed from that where they were taking her, she thought later. But it wouldn't have mattered. She would have gone anywhere the bearers of that note led her.

# EIGHT

Steve found Anne's shop dark and the door locked. His knock brought no response. As he strolled back across the street toward the hotel, he saw Smiley Birk enter the doorway ahead of him.

"Wait up!" Steve called. "I'll buy a drink."

A moment later they stood at the bar, Steve sipping whiskey and Birk staying with buttermilk. Tim Gaul was not in evidence.

Steve considered telling Birk of Anne's failure to keep her dinner date, but he decided against it. He listened to the dry rattle of chips at the tables behind him, and for a moment the synthetic hope of the Game tugged at him. He turned and saw Wiggins at one of the tables. As always, the sight of the man disgusted him; then he felt a vague pity. To decide to follow some other way of life suddenly seemed an uncomplicated thing. To decide. Somewhere in the strange meaning of that word lay the secret of existence.

The rumble of boots pulled his attention to four men who marched across the lobby to the staircase. Sheriff Illingsley was in the lead. The others were well dressed, prosperous-looking.

"Oh, oh," Smiley Birk said. "You reckon they're looking for you, Major? Or maybe your wife?"

"Who are they?"

"Judge Johnson—he's the political power in this section. Mr. Wade—he's the banker and a member of the county board. The young one is Bob Clinch—hay and grain business, president of the Star City Improvement League. A bunch of fine, upstanding, civic-minded bullyboys."

Steve smiled crookedly. "You lack respect, Deputy Birk."

Birk flashed his easy grin. He had a fringe of buttermilk on his upper lip. "They have their fun. I have mine."

Steve finished his drink and went upstairs. Male voices in Susan's room told him that Birk had guessed right about the destination of the visitors. He quickly entered his own room and stood close to the connecting door. Someone with a booming voice was paying Susan a pompous compliment. Then a crisp, high-pitched voice took over.

"The truth is, Mrs. Tanager, we know why you've come back. You're after Ben Roman's treasure."

"Good heavens!" Susan said. "Did Ben have a treasure?"

"Mrs. Tanager, I'm a banker. I know when someone is trying to bluff."

"That's very nice. But what's this about a treasure."

"Ben Roman lied on the gallows. He had money stashed somewhere. And you've come after it."

71

"If he really hid a treasure, why hasn't someone dug it up?" Susan said.

Steve chuckled inwardly. She was doing beautifully.

"*You're* the only person who knows where it is!" the thin voice said. "As a banker—"

"Yes," Susan said thoughtfully. "I can see how you might think that."

"The point is"—the booming voice now—"if you unearth such a treasure, the sheriff will be duty-bound to seize it. Stolen money."

"That would have to be proved, wouldn't it?" Susan said.

"I don't know how it could be proved or how, at this date, the rightful owners could be determined. I do know we could tie up the money for years while we tried."

"I see," Susan said pleasantly. "Then if I do know where it is, I would be foolish to dig it up. Is that what you're trying to tell me?"

Another voice made itself heard now—a young, suave voice.

"Exactly, Mrs. Tanager. Unless you were to have the cooperation of the community."

"That's nice of you, I'm sure."

"In our view, the fairest possible disposition of this loot would be to spend it on the community where it was stolen. Don't you agree, Mrs. Tanager?"

"We need a new courthouse," the booming voice put in. "A new school. The town needs a new water system . . ."

"My goodness, how much treasure is there?" Susan said.

There was a silence during which Steve pictured the

72

visitors looking at one another helplessly. Finally, the young, suave voice took over:

"The point, Mrs. Tanager, is this. If the treasure is recovered by the community, we can avoid a legal tie-up. We've decided on a plan where the funds would be shared by the county board and the town council. We would see that you got a percentage, of course."

"Fine," Susan said. "Maybe about ninety per cent?"

"We thought twenty would be generous."

This seemed a good moment for an entrance, and Steve swung open the door. Susan stood at the foot of her bed with three of the men surrounding her. The sheriff lingered near the hall door.

"This is my husband," Susan said, giving Steve a perfunctory smile. She seemed completely unruffled.

"I've been eavesdropping," Steve said. "My dear, why don't you tell these gentlemen what you told me this morning? About that mineshaft at the south end of the gulch."

"I don't remember telling you anything," Susan said.

"You said that if Ben Roman hid a treasure, that's probably where it is. It's a pretty long shot, gentlemen, but if you'll give us twenty per cent, I see no reason why you shouldn't go ahead and look."

"Steve, you're all mixed up!" Susan said "I said Ben once had an interest in some mining property down on Union Flat—Fan-tan Flat or whatever it's called now. I didn't mention a mine in the *south* end of the gulch."

Steve shrugged helplessly. "You pointed it out to me."

"Which one was it?" the man with the high-pitched voice demanded, the banker.

"Let's see. She called it the Lucky Cut."

The three men exchanged glances. Even the sheriff looked excited.

"Steve, you idiot!" Susan said. She avoided his eyes—to keep from smiling, he thought.

"Well, well!" The booming-voiced man was wringing Steve's hand. He was a paunchy, black-suited man and he held a white Stetson in his hand. He would be Judge Johnson, Steve guessed. "Perhaps this will work out for all of us."

"We want twenty per cent of what you find," Steve said.

"We'll work out an amicable settlement, I'm sure," the banker said.

He moved toward the door. The others said polite good nights and followed. Steve watched them disappear down the stairs, then closed and locked the door.

"Whew!" Susan said.

"I lied and they believed me," Steve said. "You told the truth, more or less, and they paid no attention to you."

"Have we really put them off?"

"For a while, at least."

"The name of that mine was like a magic word. What was it?"

"The Lucky Cut," Steve said. "Ben Roman had a horse hidden there the night the vigilantes took him. If he had got to it, he might have escaped."

"How could you know that?"

"I told you I got Tim Gaul to reminiscing this afternoon."

Susan sank down wearily on the bed. She had keyed herself up to deal with the callers; now she was letting down. She pulled pins out of her hair and it tumbled down her back in an ebony cascade.

"I don't like this talk about impounding the money," she said. "I certainly have an honest claim to whatever Ben Roman left. If I can get title to the property where the money is hidden, won't that give me an additional claim? What right have they to talk about confiscating it?"

"Rights aren't going to have much to do with it. Your only chance is to get the money secretly and get out of here."

"Yes," she said. She gave her hair a toss. "I must say I can't blame them much for wanting the money for the community. It's rather a noble idea."

"They're specialists in noble ideas. Politicians. Money for the community means money for them to spend. And it means votes."

She nodded soberly, thinking that bitterness was not becoming to him. She remembered Anne then and asked if he had found her. He explained about her shop being empty.

"She must have misunderstood," he said. "Probably she thought you said tomorrow night."

He had been idling about the room. Now he moved close to her. Rather timidly, he touched her hair. She met his eyes and moved her head away from his hand.

"I'd like to be alone now," she said

He lingered a moment, holding her eyes until she looked away. Then he turned abruptly to the connecting door.

There was no light in his room, and he left the door partly open till he could scratch a match and touch it to a lamp. As he did so, the door was gently shut, and he found himself standing between two men, each with his back to one of the doors. One held a cocked revolver. The other poised a teathered throwing knife. Both pressed fingers to their lips.

The man near the hall door opened it, glanced into the hall, and gestured with his head. The other, the man with the knife, stepped toward Steve and whispered, "Follow him. One word and you're dead."

Steve did as he said. The first man led the way into the hall and a few steps down it to the room across from Susan's. A lamp was burning here. The shades were drawn. Gear was scattered about the room. The man with the knife closed the door and locked it, then he patted Steve's hips and armpits to make sure he was unarmed.

The man with the gun, who was younger than the other, holstered his weapon and said, "Lay down on the bed. We'll wait till the bar closes and the night clerk hits his cot. Then we'll get out of here."

Steve lay down. The man with the knife slipped it into a scabbard sewed to his leather vest behind his right shoulder. He was dark-complected, slightly stooped, and wore a little dab of a goatee. He was mighty proud of that knife, Steve thought. The only other weapon of the kind he had seen had been carried by a Choctaw down in The Nations.

"Show him what you can do with that toothpick, Danny," the younger man said. "Just so he don't get ideas."

Danny nodded soberly. The younger man unknotted a bandanna from his neck, held it against the wall at shoulder height and dropped it. Danny's hand flashed up and out. The knife hissed through twelve feet of space and pinned the bandanna to the wall a yard above the floor.

"Convincing," Steve said.

A fancy, show-off weapon, he thought. But deadly enough—and silent.

"What's this all about?" he asked.

"Take yourself a nap," the younger man said. "We've got a long wait till closing time."

They meant to kill him, Steve supposed. They didn't want to do it in the hotel if they could avoid it. They would take him out of town to some gully where his body wouldn't be found for a while.

"Who you boys working for?"

"Shut up," Danny said. He had retrieved his weapon and returned it to its scabbard.

"We work for ourselves," the younger man said. Something about the idea seemed to amuse him. "Don't we, Danny?"

"No talking," Danny said.

"Where you from?" Steve said.

He addressed himself to the younger man and didn't see Danny move. Feathers whipped his face as the knife drove into the headboard of the bed inches above his eyes. The temptation to grab it was erased by the click of the younger man's revolver as he drew back the hammer. Sweat trickled icily down Steve's neck.

"No talking," Danny said. He swaggered over and worked the knife out of the wood.

*A show-off*, Steve thought. *He's good with that knife but shaky in the judgment department. They both are.*

The wait seemed endless. The two men played blackjack near the foot of the bed, engrossed in the fall of the cards even though they risked no money. The younger man, whose name was Ernie, rolled countless cigarettes and scuffed out the butts on the floor. Danny occasionally produced a tin of snuff and put a pinch under his lip. Steve dozed, finally. He had no idea how much time had passed when he was roused by Ernie's hand on his foot.

The door was partly open; apparently one of the pair

had checked and found the way clear. Ernie peered into the hall, patted his holstered Colt, and went out. Danny motioned for Steve to follow.

"Don't get too close to him," Danny said, touching the plumage at his shoulder. "Remember the knife is behind you."

Ernie's hand touched his gun as they reached the stairs, not gripping it but just resting on the handle. Steve walked a few steps behind him. As they neared the landing, where the stairway doubled back on itself, Steve saw his small chance and quickened his pace. He was almost within arm's length of Ernie as they made the turn to the right; for a second or two they would be around a corner from Danny.

Steve lunged, skipping a step, knocking Ernie's hand off the gun, feeling the smooth wood of the handle in his own fingers, letting his weight hit the man's back. Ernie plunged noisily downward. Steve twisted around, staggering against the balustrade. He fanned two shots upward as Danny leaped to the landing, hand raised for the knife. Danny bent in the middle, teetered, and pitched downward past Steve.

Ernie had stumbled and reeled down to the lobby but had somehow managed to keep on his feet—something of a miracle for a man in high-heeled boots. He dashed for the street door, and Steve let him go. At the moment, he had no scruples about shooting a man in the back, but he had some vague notion of catching up with Ernie later and learning who hired him.

A movement in a far corner of the dimly lighted lobby caught his eye as Ernie vanished into the street. Smiley Birk came out of the shadows, revolver in hand.

"Drop it!" Birk commanded.

Steve lowered the gun. "Dozing on the job?"

"Tanager? What goes on?"

Birk moved to the desk and turned up the low-burning lamp beside the call bell. The night clerk came timidly through a door behind the stairway and blinked stupidly as Steve bent over the figure that lay head-downward on the bottom steps.

"Dead?" Birk asked.

"Dead," Steve said. "Who is he?"

"Damned if I know," Birk said. "I never saw him before today. He's been in and out of the lobby a couple times—him and his partner." He glanced at the clerk, who stepped close, looking sick.

"I don't know him," the clerk said. "I just came on at eight."

"He was in room twenty-two," Steve said.

The clerk went to the desk and consulted the register. "Two men in there. S. Daniels and E. Smith."

"He'll be Daniels," Steve said.

"You didn't even know him?" Birk demanded.

Steve shook his head. "He and his partner took me at gunpoint and were marching me out of here."

Three or four hotel guests had drifted down to the landing. They all wore night clothes and were staring wildly. Susan pushed past them, wrapped in her kimono.

"Steve!"

"It's all right," he said.

"I heard the shooting. You weren't in your room. I—Oh, Steve!" She rushed down the steps to him and was in his arms.

Birk sent the clerk for the sheriff, who arrived within a few minutes, his trousers pulled on over a nightshirt. When he saw the dead man, he turned to look back at the

79

doorway as if to make sure he had really come through it and wasn't in bed dreaming. He surveyed the growing crowd of onlookers and finally addressed Birk.

"Who did it?"

Birk gave him a brief account of what he had seen. He had been dozing in a dark corner of the lobby and had been wakened by the shots. He had leaped to his feet as Daniels toppled down the steps past Steve and the other man dashed out of the building.

The sheriff turned to Steve with a question in his eyes.

"They took me out of my room at gunpoint," Steve said. "I have a feeling they meant to torture me for information, then probably to kill me."

"What information?"

"I told you my business here was confidential."

"All right," the sheriff said. "You're under arrest."

"No!" Susan said. "He had to do it. It's surely a case of self-defense!"

"That's pretty plainly what it was," Birk put in.

"I doubt it," the sheriff said.

# NINE

"I have no idea which lawyer to recommend," Anne Barabee said distantly. "It seems to me they're all under Judge Johnson's thumb."

They were in Anne's shop. She was sitting at the table, rapidly stitching the hem of a gray silk dress. Susan poised tensely on the edge of a chair, remembering Anne's eager friendliness of yesterday and wondering why she was so remote this morning. She had said merely that something urgent had prevented her from keeping their dinner engagement. She was quite mysterious about it.

"It's so unfair!" Susan said. "Steve was protecting himself."

"Who were the men who wanted to kill him?" It seemed an effort for Anne to keep her voice casual. She was under a strain of some sort, Susan decided—a strain she hadn't been under yesterday.

"The dead man was named Daniels; the other, Smith. Nobody seems to know anything about them."

Anne's needle faltered. She stopped sewing and aimlessly smoothed the dress.

"The dead man carried a feathered throwing knife," Susan said, seeing Anne's agitation. "Did you know him?"

Anne shook her head. "Sue, if somebody wants to kill your husband, maybe he's better off in jail. Maybe the sheriff is trying to protect him."

"I hardly think so," Susan said.

She had just come from visits with the sheriff and with Judge Johnson. Both had treated her with polite hostility. There would be an investigation. A grand jury would be given the facts. This would take time. In the meantime, Steve would be held without bail.

Anne was stitching again—a little frantically, Susan thought. There seemed to be nothing more to say, and she stood up. Anne met her eyes squarely for the first time that morning.

"Sue, I—well, I hope you don't get hurt too badly."

"Thank you."

"I"—Anne lowered her head—"I guess you might try George Crown. They say he's a good lawyer. His office is next door to the courthouse."

Susan went at once to Crown's office and found him in, but she got precious little encouragement from the visit. He was a well-barbered man with pomaded gray hair and an aura of bay rum. His frank blue eyes were sympathetic as she told of the shooting, although she had a feeling that he knew every detail already. When he questioned her about her past and her reasons for coming back to Star City, she told as much of the truth as she dared but soon found herself resorting to awkward evasions.

"If there's anything you don't want to tell me, say so," he said. "Don't lie. For a lawyer to lack information is a handicap, but for him to be misinformed is disastrous."

"I'm sorry. But it seems to me the facts of the shooting should be enough."

"Perhaps." He ran a hand lightly over his slicked-down silver hair. "I'll see what I can do, Mrs. Tanager."

Susan spent the rest of the day at the hotel, nervously awaiting word from him. It was late afternoon when she hurried to answer a soft knock on her door. But it wasn't the lawyer. It was Wiggins, who came grinning and nodding into the room.

"Look here," Susan said. "If you're seen coming here just once, it could spoil everything."

"Nobody sees what Slim Wiggins don't want seen, Mrs. Allison. I found out about that property. Abner Gill still owns it. He gave up mining and turned to ranching. Lives about eight miles from here."

"Have you seen him?"

"Been all day running that deed down. The map the county clerk showed me has lots on it but don't show cabins. I had to ride down there and figure out what lot that cabin is on."

"You'll see Mr. Gill in the morning then?"

"Figure to ride out to his ranch first thing. County clerk's guess is that he'll sell for a song. Hasn't even bothered to pay last year's taxes, which amount to a dollar thirty-five cents."

Susan took a step toward the door in an effort to end the visit, but Wiggins failed to take the hint.

"Last night I was playing cards downstairs when an idee popped into my mind," he said. "I ought to have some unsuspicious reason for wanting that cabin, it seemed like, so I went down to the flat and made an arrangement with a old Chinaman, he runs a gambling place down there. I'm going to deal a monte game for him."

It gives me a reason for wanting a cabin close by—catch on?''

"Just keep out of trouble," Susan said.

"You always hear how Chinamen save their money," Wiggins went on. "It ain't so—not all of 'em. There's places down there where they spend plenty. Opium dens and places not fitten to mention to a lady."

"Then don't," Susan said. The mere presence of this uncouth man depressed her to the point of desperation. To have to scheme with him infuriated her.

"There's Chinamen living in that cabin," Wiggins said. "I'll have to evict them out."

"Try to do it without help from the sheriff. Buy them off or something."

"Mrs. Allison, is there any chance them Chinamen might have come across the treasure accidental?"

"I think it's unlikely."

He nodded thoughtfully, reassured. He took a reluctant step toward the door, then thought of something more to say.

"That fake husband of yours got himself in bad trouble."

"It will come out all right," Susan said patiently.

"This is a mean town. Killings as might be self-defense other places are called murder here."

"You needn't concern yourself about it, Mr. Wiggins."

"It was a mistake to take up with that troublemaker, Mrs. Allison. You and me alone, we could handle this business just fine. Who was it tried to kill him?"

"I thought you might know," Susan said crisply.

"There's somebody in this we don't know about, Mrs. Allison."

84

She had been puzzling about this very thing most of the day. She had wondered if the assassins were confederates of Wiggins, but now his bewilderment seemed genuine.

"You'd better go now," she said.

He took a step toward her, holding out a hand as if to touch her. It was merely a gesture. There was something pleading in it, something pathetic, but she instinctively retreated. He seemed about to speak, but quick footsteps in the hall prompted him to hold his tongue. There was a brisk rapping on the door.

Susan pointed to the door of Steve's room, and Wiggins made for it. She hissed after him, "You get clear away from here as soon as I open my door."

The caller turned out to be the young, smooth-talking man who had been with the judge and the banker the night before. She smiled politely and stepped aside so he could come in.

"Mr. Clinch, isn't it?" she said. "The Improvement League president?"

"I think we have something to talk about, Mrs. Tanager," he said, clutching his hat in front of him. "I've been up at the Lucky Cut all day."

The absurdity of this eager young man poking around a deserted mine struck Susan funny and she had to smile. "I told you you'd find nothing there."

"I'm not in a patient mood, Mrs. Tanager. I want to be told everything you know about the treasure. You're in no position to bargain."

Susan's smile faded. "If I know half as much as you seem to think, I'd say I'm in an excellent position to bargain."

"Not with your husband in jail."

"Does that have something to do with buried treasure?"

"The Improvement League has considerable political
influence, Mrs. Tanager. Considerable. I'm sure I could
persuade the authorities to speed up the investigation. If
your husband is not guilty of murder, he would be released—well, at once."

Anger wrenched at her, but she pretended not to understand what Clinch was getting at. She said, "That would
be very nice of you."

"I have no intention of doing this until the community
is assured of getting Ben Roman's money."

"Oh." Susan couldn't trust herself to say more. She
wanted to tell Mr. Clinch that he was an extorting little rat,
but she took a deep breath and held her tongue.

"You must agree that my position is an unselfish one,"
Clinch said piously. "My only concern is for the community."

Susan closed her eyes, still struggling with her temper.
A small sound from the next room reached her ears, and
she realized Wiggins was in there, listening to every word.
Frustration bore in on her. She found herself thinking of
Steve, wishing for his strength.

"That mine is dangerous," Clinch said. "The shor-
ing is rotten. If we send a crew up there and start digging
every which way, there's likely to be an ugly accident."

"Last night in your eagerness and greed you allowed
my husband to mislead you, Mr. Clinch. Now let me say
as plainly as I can that there is no hidden treasure in the
Lucky Cut. If anyone gets hurt poking around there, the
fault will be yours."

"All right. Then where—"

"I have nothing more to say to you." Susan stepped to the door and flung it open.

Clinch hesitated, then gave her a curt nod and marched into the hall.

"Just remember you refused to co-operate with the community," he said.

Susan closed the door behind him, marched to the other door, and flung it open on Wiggins.

"I told you—" She was too furious to go on. "Just get out of here, please. Now."

She saw then that Wiggins was as angry as she was. He said, "What was that all about? I want to know."

She explained as quickly as she could. Wiggins listened tensely, suspiciously.

"I've gave considerable time and money to this business," he said. "This treasure is my life work, you might say. You try to cheat me and you know what I'll do."

"Yes. I won't cheat you."

"I'll ruin you and your family. And I'll kill you."

Finally, he left. She was in too much of a state to sit and wait for Mr. Crown any longer. She threw a shawl over her shoulders and left the room.

She felt the stares of the clerk and the loungers as she crossed the lobby to the street door. The worst had happened, she thought. The whole of Star City knew who she was and why she had come back. She couldn't take two steps without being observed. Everything depended on Wiggins now, and he had turned nasty. She had one decisive advantage, of course; she alone knew exactly where the treasure was. Wiggins could dig and search and tear the cabin down without much chance of finding it.

She found George Crown tidying his desk before locking up his office.

"I planned to pay you a call on my way home," he said. "Judge Johnson and I have been shouting at each other most of the afternoon." He paused as if to give her time to appreciate him as a man who could shout at Judge Johnson. "When I insisted that he set bail, he did. Twenty thousand dollars!"

"That's—preposterous!"

"Of course. The judge knows that better than anyone. He and his cronies want the Roman treasure. They're going to put all the pressure on you they can."

"I've had a taste of it," Susan said.

She told him about the visit from Mr. Bob Clinch. Crown listened gravely. Suddenly, he asked, "Do you really know where the treasure is hidden?"

"You, too?"

He smiled. "I'm curious, naturally."

"I hired you to get Steve out of jail."

"Of course you did." He wagged his silver head sadly. "They can't make the charge against Major Tanager stick, Mrs. Tanager. The judge is bluffing. That's about the only reassuring thing I can say at this time. The trouble is— well, the effort to get this loot for the community is going to be mighty popular. The judge can stall for weeks, if necessary, without much danger of arousing public opinion."

"While Steve sits in jail."

"That's about it. You see, Mrs. Tanager, you can hardly expect to find—uh, sympathy here."

"I don't expect to. Have you seen Steve?"

"Yes, and he wasn't very helpful. He tells a straight story about the shooting, but I couldn't get much else out of him. Incidentally, he said to tell you not to come to see him. He said just to sit tight and not worry."

# TEN

Tim Gaul's cabin atop Sunrise Ridge had windows in three sides and the door in the other. By shifting a rickety stool and a battered telescope from door to north and south windows, Tim could peer omnisciently at the town, the focusing roads, and a large part of the gulch. Today, however, he spent a good bit of the time perched at the east window, which commanded the monotonous rolling country behind the ridge.

This was grassland, a sea of hilltops that receded into Madison Valley, and it served a handful of ranchers as summer range. Tim watched a hawk trace its stealthy circle, drop, and rise again. Once, a few longhorns drifted into view. A stray wind lifted a dust devil. At last, another spot of motion caught his eye, and he focused the glass on it.

It was a rider, still miles away but headed straight for town. Even through the glass, horse and man were little bigger than an ant; but Tim had watched the same man leave town earlier in the morning, and he knew it was Slim Wiggins.

Wiggins had been around in the wild days. For all his bumpkinesque qualities, he was known to Tim as a sly, shrewd man. He had, in fact, been of some help to Tim, having been willing to tell what he knew of certain desperadoes in order to persuade the vigilantes that he was on the side of justice. He had come back to Star City from time to time—though this was a chronological nicety that escaped Tim—and he had shown very little interest in anything except gambling. Certainly he had never been one to gallivant around the country on horseback. Yesterday he had visited Fan-tan Flat, just as the Tanagers had the day before. He had also made two trips to the courthouse. And this morning he had ridden off into country where there was nothing but Ab Gill's little spread and maybe a line camp or so. Now, with the sun high overhead, he was returning and he was in one hell of a hurry.

Tim could see no connection between Wiggins' activities and the other strange things that were going on in town, but he took it for granted there was one. Night before last, Anne Barabee had ridden away at dusk in the company of two men. Tim had worried a bit about her, but the next morning she was back in her shop. Yesterday afternoon she, too, had visited the courthouse. Then she had hired a horse and ridden off cross-country in the same direction Wiggins had taken this morning.

Near as Tim could figure it, the same two strangers who had ridden off with Anne must have come back in an hour or so and tried to abduct Major Tanager, who had blasted one of them to kingdom come. Tim was inclined to consider this an admirable piece of work on the part of the major—for whom he had a friendly feeling since the major had taken the trouble to sit down and have a talk. But the major was in jail. Bill Illingsley had turned a deaf ear to Tim's protest that a man who toted a feathered knife was plainly a killer and deserved just what he had got.

Tim spent very little time trying to make these events fit together. To him, they signified just one thing—a return of the enemies he hated with all his being. He had only to watch and wait, to keep track of key people. Eventually, the pattern of their behavior would become clear; no sense in trying to ponder it out now. What he pondered about was where he could get some lumber for a gallows. It would be nice to have one ready, he thought.

Wiggins was riding hard. When he was still a good mile away, Tim put away the telescope and set out for town, bending into the torso-forward walk that folks said he got from scooting up and down the ridge several times a day. His course now was straight downhill, and in five minutes he was loitering in front of the hotel, watching Wiggins top a low shoulder of the ridge and ride into the road that led into Center Street. Tim expected him to take his exhausted horse to the livery, but he left the animal at the hotel hitching-rack and hurried past Tim into the building.

Tim followed, glaring at the clerk and pausing till Wiggins was beyond the turn in the stairway. It was plain enough that a man wouldn't be in such a rush just to be by himself in his room; Wiggins was going to see somebody, and Tim wanted to know whom. He went up the steps quietly, stopping as soon as he had a view of the second-floor hallway. Wiggins was in front of Mrs. Tanager's door. As Tim watched, it opened and Wiggins pushed into the room.

Tim returned to the lobby and sat down, enjoying a grim satisfaction. Even though he had no idea what Wiggins

91

could be up to, another fragment of the puzzle had dropped into place. Wiggins and Ben Roman's widow were up to something together.

Wiggins was flushed and out of breath. There was a murderous resentment in his face. Susan had the feeling that when he spoke he was going to shout, but he managed to control his voice, if not his words. When she had closed the door and stood with her back against it, he even managed a thin and insecure smile.

"Mrs. Allison, you're trying to cheat me."

"Look here," Susan said. "I won't have you bursting in this way. Did you buy the property?"

His eyes bored into her. "You pretending you don't know Anne Barabee bought it out from under me?"

"Anne Barabee *what?*" She tried to shake off a feeling of catastrophe. "There's some mistake, Mr. Wiggins."

He seized her by the shoulders and searched her face. "You didn't put her up to it?"

She met his eyes for a moment, angrily, fearfully. Then she knocked his hands away and stepped back. Fighting for calmness, she said, "I did not! Now tell me what happened."

"I rode out to buy that property from Gill, like I told you I would. Anne Barabee was out there last night and bought it. She had a deed all made out, and Gill signed it. She give him a hundred dollars."

Susan caught her breath. "How could Anne possibly know about it?"

"You told her. That's the only way."

"I told her?" Susan said heatedly. She rejected the suspicion that crossed her mind then. Wiggins seemed

92

altogether too upset to be acting. "Anne could have gone to the courthouse and learned what property you asked about."

"That don't explain nothing. How would she know we were working together? Only I and you know that. And the major."

Susan sat down on the bed and tried to think. "I would have nothing to gain by bringing Anne into this, Mr. Wiggins. You can put that out of your head."

"You could have some scheme to freeze me out."

"That's ridiculous. I can't freeze you out. You know that."

Wiggins' expression softened as he studied her now. His head moved in a series of barely perceptible little nods. He took an idle step toward the window, then spun around and pointed a finger at her.

"There's somebody else in this. Who, Mrs. Allison?"

"There can't be. Only my sister knows I've come back here. You know we can rule her out."

She was suddenly terribly frightened. There was somebody else, all right. There had to be. Those two men who had tried to abduct Steve were surely after the treasure. That citizen's committee, or whatever it was, was after it. But how could any of these possibly know that Wiggins was to buy the property on which it was hidden?

"I think I'd better have a talk with Anne," Susan said.

"I'm the one to do that," Wiggins said. "It'd be the natural thing for a man who's had a piece of property bought out from under him. You go running to her, you'll give the whole show away for sure."

Susan saw that there was some sense to this. "All right, neither of us will see her. We'll do nothing till I've talked to Steve."

Wiggins seemed about to protest, but he set his jaw and nodded reluctantly.

"From the way you've talked, that treasure ain't going to be easy to find," he muttered hopefully.

"It isn't."

"Well, that's one advantage in our favor."

Wiggins kept turning to the window as if he could think better when not looking at her. He was still visibly upset, but at least his anger no longer focused on her. How lonely he must be, she thought, this strange ugly creature who lived by cheating and never learned that we make our own loneliness. Her moment of pity faded when he faced her again.

"You got to be almighty careful," he said. "You could be made to tell where that treasure is. Somebody might try it."

He spoke softly, with something like concern for her in his voice—but with something unpleasant in it, too. He was as much intrigued by the idea as alarmed by it, she thought.

The jail was a two-story stone building in back of the courthouse. The downstairs was one large untidy room furnished with a cot for the jailer, a desk, a table, a few chairs, and a cookstove. The cell block was upstairs.

Susan found the pockmarked little jailer ladling stew into a tin plate. She gave him the pass the sheriff had written and waited while he held it at arm's length and puzzled out the words.

"Never did have a prisoner got so many visitors," he said. "You being a woman, it wouldn't be fitting to search you, I guess. Set at that table, and I'll bring him down."

She obeyed. In a minute or two, Steve came down the stairs followed by the jailer. Steve sat across the table from her. The jailer shoved the plate of stew in front of him, muttering that he might as well eat his dinner while it was hot.

"That's some lawyer you got me," Steve said. "He lectured me an hour yesterday about my moral duty to see that the Roman money goes to the community."

"Yes," Susan said. "I'm afraid he's playing the judge's game."

"As if *I* knew where the money is."

The jailer dished himself a plate of stew and sat down at the roller-top desk to eat it. This was in a far corner of the room and he turned his chair sideways so he could keep an eye on his prisoner.

"I've had other visitors, too," Steve said. "Wade, the banker. And that Improvement League sprout."

"Mr. Clinch. He was around to see me, too."

The jailer seemed engrossed in his meal. Susan lowered her voice to a whisper and told about Anne's buying the property before Wiggins got to the owner. Steve put down his fork and listened incredulously.

"It must be the judge and his bunch who are behind Anne," she said. "Who else could it be? But why would they pick Anne to front for them? And how could they know about Wiggins?"

Steve toyed with his stew unappreciatively. "Well, somebody knows. Unless Wiggins is double-dealing us himself."

"I hardly think so. What would he gain by throwing in with Anne? And he was horribly upset when he found she had bought the cabin. I can't believe he was pretending."

"I suppose the judge could have hired that pair of

beauties who tried to march me out of the hotel, too . . . That thought is enough to make a man lose his temper.''

His smile made Susan feel better. She said, ''I think it's unlikely they'll find the hiding place—whoever they are.''

''If that's true, we can beat them. The first thing is to find out who they are. Have Wiggins watch that property day and night. Tell him to move into that neighboring cabin.''

The jailer had finished his meal. ''Visit's over.''

Steve pushed away his plate and stood up. ''Have the hotel send over some decent food, will you?'' he said, smiling again. As he turned toward the stairs, he threw her a kiss.

She left the jail smiling and with the feeling that treasure hunting was, after all, a game. Even though the play turned deadly, you didn't forget how to smile for those you—for your friends. Steve was good for her, she thought.

George Crown's office was next door to the courthouse, and she stopped in. The lawyer sprang up from his desk and held a chair for her, but she shook her head.

''My husband thinks you're more interested in lecturing him on his moral duty than in getting him out of jail,'' she said.

Crown smiled professionally and made a helpless little gesture. ''I suppose he's right. The judge is behaving deplorably—even the county prosecutor has told him so. Yet I agree with his objective. That road-agent loot belongs to this county, Mrs. Tanager.''

Susan opened her handbag. ''How much do I owe you, Mr. Crown?''

Surprise touched him briefly, then he made the helpless gesture again. "I've been worth exactly nothing to you."

"You put in some time."

She laid a goldpiece on the desk. He quickly picked it up and dropped it back into her bag. "I have the vestiges of a conscience," he said.

She turned to leave and almost collided with the plump, breathless figure of Judge Johnson in the doorway.

"Glad I caught you here!" the judge boomed. "I'd like a word with you and your attorney."

"Have you decided to do your own extorting?" Susan looked him straight in the eye. "Last time you sent Mr. Clinch."

The judge flushed, swallowed hard, and decided to be amused. He managed a chuckle.

"Well, well!" he said, turning to Crown. "The lady admits to having something worth extorting. That's more than she's done heretofore."

Crown smiled dutifully.

"That's certainly an unwarranted conclusion," Susan said.

"Mrs. Tanager," the judge said. "This is a gold town. The prospect of a rich haul stirs the old fever in us. We're apt to lose our heads."

"And your principles."

The judge again ignored her and addressed himself to Crown. "Bob Clinch believes we were misled about the treasure being in the Lucky Cut. He—"

"You certainly were!" Susan said.

"Bob says that even if it's there, finding it will be dangerous, expensive, and time-consuming. He thinks the community ought to offer your client a full fifty per cent in return for her information."

97

"She's not my client," Crown said. "If she were, I'd advise her that that is a handsome offer."

"In view of the certainty that the money will be impounded if the community doesn't benefit, I would say it is more than handsome," the judge said.

"Let Steve out of jail," Susan said. "Then come to me with your offers."

"My dear young lady," the judge said righteously, "your husband killed a man. You can't bargain with me for his freedom."

"Nonsense! Mr. Clinch made it clear that I could."

"I imagine Bob Clinch offered you whatever assistance his organization could give. Provided, that is—"

"You know very well what he offered me, Judge," Susan said. "You pompous hypocrite!"

The judge's mouth fell open. He turned beet-red. His lips moved futilely a time or two before he could make them form words.

"That—from Ben Roman's woman!"

Susan was on the verge of an outburst she knew she would regret. The judge, she thought, was on the verge of apoplexy. She managed a cold little smile and flounced out of the office.

As she walked back toward the hotel, she gave in to an impulse and crossed the street to Anne Barabee's shop. But the door was locked, and she could raise no one.

# ELEVEN

Sheriff Bill Illingsley lay on his stomach at the crest of the spur above Fan-tan Flat. The sun was blistering hot on his back, the ground bake-oven warm on his underside, and he was of the opinion that he would be more comfortable on the south slope of hell. Chin on hands, spectacles pushed to his forehead, he patiently kept his eyes on the cabins below.

Lately he had been paying more attention to Tim Gaul's tips than he would admit to anyone—especially to Tim. The old vigilante, of course, was obsessed by a fear of an outlaw organization that he himself had put out of business. He was likely to read wild meanings into things he saw through that damn spyglass of his. But if you considered the bare facts and drew your own conclusions, Tim's information was sometimes worth looking into.

His tip about those cabins down there, for instance, was mighty interesting. The Chinese occupants had moved out and a white man had moved into each. One of these men was Slim Wiggins, who seemed to be doing his gambling Chinese-style these days. The older man Tim couldn't identify for sure but had some suspicions about, probably fanciful. Bill knew, of course, that the Tanagers had shown some interest in this part of the flat, day after they arrived in town. The odds seemed pretty good that all this added up to something.

Bill Illingsley had dreamed wild dreams with the best of them in the old days. He'd hit heavy color, too—for a few brief weeks he'd felt like a rich man. He and a partner had taken somewhere around ten thousand dollars out of a fifty-foot claim in the upper gulch before the pay petered out. They had holed up for the winter in a sluice-lumber shack with the gold dust under the floor and one or the other always on guard with a shotgun.

One evening when Bill had ridden to town for beans and tobacco, four men had riddled the shack from two sides with Henry rifles. When Bill got back, the walls looked like colanders and his partner like he had been put through one. The gold was gone.

Bill had joined the vigilantes shortly after that. He had absorbed some of Tim Gaul's passion for righteous vengeance. When the vigilance committee had set up courts and law-enforcement machinery, he had run for sheriff and got elected. He had given the town and the county the kind of rigid regulation that the crime-sickened people wanted, and he had held the office ever since.

He thought mostly in terms of politics now, playing along with Judge Johnson's bunch, cherishing the respect of the voters, planning to run for county treasurer when the time was ripe. The uncertainties of political life plagued him, however; he had saved nothing from his salary and fees against the day when he would lose an election

Sometimes he pictured himself becoming another Tim Gaul—who lived by hunting and, except for the bounty he collected from wolf pelts, seldom saw cash. At such pessimistic moments, Bill recalled his stolen gold with a sudden blinding bitterness.

If there was a treasure, he thought, five thousand dollars worth of it belonged to him. If he should happen to be the one to find it, he couldn't see that stashing away about twenty troy pounds of it would strain his conscience much. In spite of the judge's windy talk of impoundment and such, Bill gathered that the money would pretty clearly be the property of the finder. To turn it over to the community short only what had been stolen from him would still be an act of generosity. A man might even take a little interest money.

Because of this trend of thought and because he didn't like to admit to taking Tim's tips seriously, Bill hadn't mentioned to anyone where he was going to spend the afternoon. He had even gone to some pains to keep Tim away from his telescope, giving him a dollar of county money to relieve Smiley Birk in keeping an eye on Mrs. Tanager.

Every hour or so, Bill crept back down the slope to where his horse was grazing, had a drink from his canteen, and cooled off in the shade of a boulder. When he returned to the crest after one such respite, he saw that a man had come out of the farther of the cabins, had led a horse out of the lean-to at the far end of the building, and was saddling up.

Bill had brought no field glasses, but he was pretty sure the man was nobody he knew. He was of slender build and seemed to be young. The back of his faded denim shirt was dark with sweat, and he kept wiping his face with a

101

bandanna. Before he rode off, he went into the cabin and came out buckling on a gunbelt. Tim's guess just might be right, Bill decided—this could be the man who had registered at the hotel as E. Smith, the companion of the man Tanager had killed. If so, the lad had got himself another revolver somewhere.

Instead of heading east toward the stage road, the man jogged straight into the neck of the flat and began to work his way into the hills to the northwest. This was mildly strange. There was nothing over that way but the Black-tails and bad riding.

Bill Illingsley weighed the situation and knew that he had to have a look inside that cabin, even though that meant possible observation by Wiggins from the other building—which was maybe a hundred yards this side. Bill got his horse and led the animal zigzag down the steep slope.

The cabin door had no lock. Bill pushed it open and stepped inside. Having spent most of the afternoon in bright sunlight, he found the interior dark as night. Something warned him—perhaps the smell of fresh earth. He stood motionless until his eyes began to adjust. He saw then that half the floor had been torn up and that he was standing on the brink of a freshly dug, grave-deep hole.

There were two rooms in the cabin, separated by a log partition. The connecting doorway was to Bill's right, adjacent to the outer wall, and he picked his way to it. The floor in the second, smaller room was still intact. The floor boards from the other room had been piled against the wall. Bill went back for another look at the excavation.

The sides and bottom of the hole were square and even; there was no evidence of any large object having been dug out. And Bill was certain that the man who had ridden away had carried no burden with him. Well, it was plain enough that somebody believed Ben Roman's loot was here somewhere. The next step was to find out who.

Bill rode to the end of the flat at a lope and reined into the hills. The man who had left the cabin a few minutes earlier had chosen the easiest slopes without thought of concealing his tracks. He was headed for the Blacktail buttes, it seemed. Suddenly a cog clicked in Bill Illingsley's memory.

"Road Agents' Roost!" he said aloud.

This was an almost inaccessible cabin hidden in a patch of pine high on the northern butte. No one knew who had built it or when. Tim Gaul had discovered it after the vigilante cleanup. Since the town could be seen clearly from it, the cabin was believed to have been a lookout station for road agents. When a stagecoach set out with gold aboard, it was said, a spy in town put wet grass in his stove to make a smoke signal. The bandits in the cabin then descended and held up the coach.

There was no game on the butte, so the cabin was never visited by hunters and was now half-forgotten. Bill had been there only once, out of curiosity, and he remembered the place was mighty difficult to get to.

When he reached a draw at the bottom of the butte, he caught a glimpse of his quarry—on foot and about three-quarters of the way up to the pines that hid the cabin. Bill waited till the man reached the trees; then he found the trail and urged his horse upward.

The butte was mostly black rock, with enough soil in places for a patchy beard of pine. The trail wound and plunged and hairpinned. Some of it was along ledges where the sheriff dismounted and led his horse. After a few minutes, he came unexpectedly to a shelf and a cuplike depression about half an acre in area. Here, two horses nibbled at a mottling of grass. One was saddled—that of the man Bill was following. The other was a sleek, long-coupled roan Bill had never seen before.

He left his own mount here and set out on foot for the last part of the climb. The distance to the pines was not great, but the trail led almost straight up and the footing was mighty poor in places. Bill took his time, wishing for better cover. He couldn't see the cabin among the trees, but he was pretty sure he could be seen from it.

When he reached the pines, he sat down to get his breath and to study the small section of log wall that was now visible through the foliage. After a minute or two, he stole to the end of the cabin and put his ear to it. He was pretty sure there were two men inside; there should have been talking, but he heard nothing. Ducking under a window, he made his way to the door and listened again. He was not a man who scared easily, but the silence stirred terror in him. Whoever was in there must have seen him coming and was waiting for him. For the first time, he wished he hadn't come alone.

He drew his Colt and flattened himself against the wall beside the door. He drew a deep breath and called out:

"County sheriff out here! Come out with your hands in sight!"

The door immediately scraped open. The man he had followed stood before him, smiling insolently.

"What you want, Sheriff?"

"What's your name?"

"Smith."

"Who else is in there?"

"Nobody. Just me and the pack rats."

"Turn around."

Smith obeyed with a cockiness that Bill didn't like. Bill gingerly relieved him of his revolver.

"I'll have a look inside," Bill said.

He stepped cautiously into the cabin behind Smith. The dark, one-room building seemed empty except for the two of them. Then Bill saw the small loft at the far end. There was room for a man to lie up there in the darkness. He walked under it and pointed both his gun and Smith's upward.

"All right, up there! Come down with your hands in sight!"

There was no reply, no sound at all. Smith waited tensely, expectantly.

"I'm going to count three," Bill said. "Then I'm going to shoot up through the floor."

He didn't see the knothole slightly behind his head. Or the gun muzzle in it.

The explosion shook the cabin. Dust that had been accumulating for nearly a decade sifted down from the loft and settled on Bill Illingsley's prone and lifeless body.


A deputy found the sheriff's horse tied in front of the courthouse the next morning. A few minutes later, a storekeeper found Bill's body in an alley. Part of his skull had been blown away. At first, he was thought to have taken his own life. But there was no blood on the ground around him, and the coroner figured out that the bullet had been fired from above—at an angle that made suicide most unlikely.

By eight o'clock, the whole town had the news. Stern-faced men began to gather in front of the courthouse. Tim Gaul came down from his hilltop, had a look at the sheriff's body, and went back up for his shotgun. No one joked about this; today folks regarded Tim without condescension. Some opined that he had been right all along: the Roman gang was coming to life again. One or two even asked him if the vigilantes would ride again. Tim merely nodded in reply, not quite trusting himself to speak up yet.

Late in the morning, the county board held a meeting. Smiley Birk was made acting sheriff until an election could be held. He was not the senior deputy, but his appointment was considered wise from a political viewpoint. He was an extremely popular man. He was more than ordinarily handy with a gun, and folks knew this. If he lacked reverence for politics and politicians, the commissioners (and Judge Johnson) were sure that a taste of authority would change that.

The first thing Birk did was to get his deputies busy trying to trace Bill Illingsley's movements the afternoon before. The next thing was to make a little speech to the crowd in front of the courthouse, persuading it to disperse. The third thing was to let Steve Tanager out of jail.

"I've talked to the county prosecutor," he said as he unlocked Steve's cell. "I gave him the straight of it, and he's dropping charges. The judge ain't going to like it, but he can't do a damn thing about it if the prosecutor won't prosecute."

Birk led the way downstairs and waited while the jailer returned Steve's wallet, watch, and pocketknife.

"If you have any ideas about Illingsley's murder, I'd like to hear them," Birk said.

"How would I know anything about that?" Steve said.

"I figure the man you killed and the other lad were aiming to take you out of town and make you tell what you know. I figure you have a pretty good idea who they're working for. It seems like the same crowd might've got Bill.''

''If I could put you on to this 'crowd,' I think I'd do it,'' Steve said. ''But I never saw those men before, Smiley, and I don't know who they might have been working for.''

Birk took a breath and blew it out noisily. ''Would your wife know?''

Steve frowned. ''I don't think so.''

''You're not completely sure?''

''What makes you think Illingsley was killed by—treasure hunters? He must've had his share of enemies.''

''He wasn't an easy man to get along with,'' Birk conceded. ''But I can't think of anybody who'd want to put a bullet in him.''

They walked together to the sheriff's office. Birk extended his hand and Steve took it warmly.

''Thanks, Smiley.''

''I hope you find your damn treasure,'' Birk said, flashing his wide grin. ''I'll be watching like a hawk.''

''So you can impound it?''

''Seems likely. But all I want right now is Bill's killer.''

On his way to the hotel, Steve saw Tim Gaul moving parallel along the walk across the street. Steve waved jauntily. When he reached the hotel, he waved again and motioned for Tim to join him.

Tim approached with a certain reticence. The shotgun was under his arm.

''They let me out,'' Steve said.

''Man that carries a throwing knife is a bad one,'' Tim said. ''Deserves to die.''

''Come inside.'' Steve touched Tim's arm. ''I'll stand a drink.''

107

"With thanks to you, I'll say no. They killed Bill Illingsley last night."

"I heard. *Who* killed him, Tim?"

Tim was startled by the question. He muttered, "They got Jase Nooner down in Idaho. Now Bill."

*"Who?"* Steve persisted.

"We let too many slip through our fingers. They're coming back. We got to clean them out."

"You let Luke Lumby slip through your fingers. Who else?"

"Lumby was the worst. As soon shoot you as look at you."

*The same might be said of you*, Steve thought. Tim had clearly passed the point where he could judge objectively. Any killing that he did now would seem just to him— merely because he did it.

"Tell me about Lumby," Steve said.

Tim studied him critically. Again, Steve touched his arm and suggested they go inside. Tim still refused a drink, but they went into the lobby and found chairs in a quiet corner.

"Lumby ran the stage-robbing part of the gang," Tim said. "He was recognized at two, three holdups. The only law we had was Ben Roman's mining-district court. When Luke was arrested, Ben said he had no jurisdiction over criminal cases. He cussed Luke out and let him go.

"Oh, they had an organization! They had spies all over town so they'd know when gold was shipped. They even had a lookout cabin up on the north butte. Nobody knew it was there till I found it after—I forget just when. Found a trail beside a boulder at the head of a little draw at the foot of the butte. Chokeberry so thick you'd never know the rock was there . . ."

"What did Lumby look like?" Steve asked.

"Like the murderin' devil he was!" Tim struggled with the details of a description. "Young, he was—not more'n twenty-five. Smallish. Wore high heels on his boots. Darkish hair. Had a fancy mustache and a beard trimmed to a point—one of those imperials, they call 'em."

"Tell me more about him," Steve said. "What were his habits?"

"Bad," Tim said, a fleck of humor in his faded eyes.

"Liquor? Gambling?"

"Robbing stagecoaches," Tim said.

"What about women? Wasn't Anne Barabee his girl?"

"It's said they planned to marry. You through asking questions?"

"No," Steve said. "Tell me about Slim Wiggins. He was here in the old days, wasn't he?"

"The old days?" Uncertainty fluttered in the creases of Tim's face as he fought his chronic battle with time. "I guess you'd say so. A tinhorn, Wiggins. A weasel."

"This Bob Clinch—the Improvement League man. Was he here in the old days?"

Tim looked puzzled. "What's that to you?"

"Did he ride with your vigilantes?"

"Bob Clinch? He must've come along later."

"Did Judge Johnson ride with you?"

"The membership of the vigilantes is secret," Tim asserted.

"I'll take that as an affirmative answer," Steve said.

"Take it as you damn well please," Tim said, suddenly hostile. "If you're going to answer your own questions, the hell with you."

The old vigilante stood up. Steve clapped him on the shoulder and got a narrow look in return. Tim recklessly

109

swung the shotgun up under his arm and headed for the street.

Steve crossed the lobby to the stairway. The ugly memory of Daniels' death rose in him as he mounted the steps. Then he remembered how Susan had rushed into his arms that night, and the ugliness was erased. He took the steps two at a time.

# TWELVE

She was wearing her kimono and she opened the door a
cautious inch at first, flinging it wide when she saw Steve.
She was utterly surprised, and he took advantage of the
moment to draw her to him. She responded up to a point,
saying his name over and over again, her hands pressing
his broad back, her body against him in eager welcome.
But she turned her cheek to his kiss.

"Thank heaven you're out of that awful place!" She
tried gently to move away. He held her tightly.

"The jail was all right. It was being away from you that
was awful."

"That's very gallant," she said tartly. "But please—
let's not be carried away by your homecoming."

"Susan, we're fifteen hundred miles from Cedar
Rapids."

"And we have a business arrangement," she said.

He released her, and they moved on into the room. He
explained that Smiley Birk had freed him.

111

"I expect it's going to be a shock to Judge Johnson," he said.

"To a lot of people," Susan said. "I've had calls from the mayor, a minister, a schoolteacher, and Mrs. Bob Clinch. They all called attention to pressing community needs. They all managed to hint that if I would co-operate with the community, Judge Johnson would co-operate with you. I must say, though, that they were less crass about it than the judge himself."

"*Mrs.* Bob Clinch?"

Susan nodded with exaggerated solemnity. "She invited me to tea this afternoon. I was just dressing."

"I suppose that in Star City an invitation from Mrs. Clinch is quite a social plum."

"It's pretty ridiculous. I'm sure that under ordinary circumstances she'd rather die than have Ben Roman's widow in her house."

Steve laughed. "Ben Roman's widow and the present wife of a jailbird."

She cocked her head whimsically. "The traveling companion of a jailbird. What if she knew that!"

They were standing self-consciously apart, making conversation like nervous youngsters, he thought. Would it be so awful for her if he took her into his arms and loved her—now? Couldn't this time away from her home be something separate from the rest of her life—a brief and meaningful life in itself?

*Not for her*, he decided, *or for me. If she ever comes to me fully, without reservations, it's forever. She knows that, and I know it. And she's determined it shan't be . . . Forget her, then. You owe her nothing.*

"Steve, do they know who killed the sheriff?"

"No."

"Do they think it could have anything to do with the treasure?"

"Birk thinks so."

She sank down on the bed, looking frightened. "First, old Jase Nooner. Then that queer man you killed. Now the sheriff. Steve, what have I done?"

"Damn damnation!" he said. "Don't take the sins of the world on yourself."

She regarded him reflectively. "May I ask you something? Didn't killing that man bother you at all?"

"Killing him, yes—his death, not at all," Steve said, surprised that he could answer so readily. He added gravely, "Killing tears something inside me. I even hate to hunt."

"You don't seem to have any trouble living with your conscience. That's what I mean."

"A soldier learns to do that quickly enough. You don't let yourself pity the thing you kill. You may respect it, even love it, but you must refuse it pity."

This was a thing he had never discussed before. There was much more that he wanted to say and couldn't because he didn't understand it himself. It had to do with the war, with dreams and failures, with retreat to the uncomplicated challenge of the Game. And with a man's need for something more than all of these. Something? . . .

"Some *one*," he said, answering himself aloud. Susan looked at him strangely, and he said quickly, "You mustn't be late for Mrs. Clinch's party. And I want a bath and a change of clothes."

The Clinch home was a large, white, two-story building balanced on a knoll where it overlooked the town. A pretty

Swedish girl answered Susan's knock. Young, doll-like Mrs. Clinch stood on a footstool in the parlor. Anne Barabee knelt at her feet and pinned up the hem of a green striped dress. Anne looked up wide-eyed, as startled as Susan.

"We'll be finished in a minute," Mrs. Clinch said when greetings were over. Susan selected a chair and said not to hurry. She wondered if Anne's being here was purely coincidental. She decided it couldn't be anything else.

"I stopped by your shop once or twice," she said. "Your door was locked."

"I'm out a good deal," Anne mumbled, her mouth full of pins.

"We keep her busy," Mrs. Clinch said. "Anne does keep up with the styles."

When the hem was pinned, Mrs. Clinch left the room to change to another dress. Anne fussed silently with the contents of her sewing bag.

"Steve's out of jail," Susan said. This struck her as a ridiculous way to begin a conversation and she had to smile.

Anne dropped her sewing bag and turned her back as she picked it up. When she faced Susan, her jaw was set hard and her eyes shone.

"I wish he weren't!" she burst out. "He—he was safe there. Oh, I wish you'd get on the next stage and never come back!"

"Anne," Susan said calmly. "I'd like to know exactly why you wish that."

"Major Tanager is in danger. Isn't that plain enough?"

"No. It's very obscure."

Anne gestured violently. "He's a dangerous man.

114

There are people who want him out of the way so they'll have just you to deal with. Surely you know they killed the sheriff.''

"They?''

"Don't ask me who, Sue. Just listen to me. When I came to see you that day, I wanted to be your friend. That's *all* I wanted. Then everything changed. I *had* to buy that property. My future—my whole life—''

Susan saw an opportunity to bluff and seized it. "What property?''

"Why—the cabin Wiggins was to buy for you.''

"Wiggins?'' Susan stared blankly. "Anne, what on earth are you talking about? Who is Wiggins?''

Anne wasn't taken in. "Sue, you needn't pretend. I know that Wiggins is in with you. I know a good bit more about you, too!''

Susan shook her head hopelessly, sticking to her guns. "I simply don't know what you're talking about.''

"Deny everything if you want to,'' Anne said viciously. "What are you going to do when your Major Tanager gets himself killed? Are you going to play the part of a grieving widow?''

The insinuation was obvious. Anne knew that she wasn't married to Steve. Susan made a supreme effort to conceal her shock. "You're terribly frightened of something, aren't you, Anne?''

"Terribly,'' Anne admitted. "Oh, Sue, all I want is to get out of here. Forever.''

"You've hinted that you know who killed the sheriff. Mightn't you have warned him?''

"No! I didn't know! I'm trying to warn you now, Sue. At least give me credit for that.''

The Swedish girl and another woman came into the

room. The woman, gray-faced, tastelessly dressed, turned out to be Mrs. Wade, the wife of the banker. She had come to tea, too.

Mrs. Clinch appeared simultaneously with the arrival of a third guest—the plump and smiling wife of Judge Johnson. Anne folded the dress with the pinned hem into her bag and left the gathering.

It seemed to Susan that the company had been picked to put her under the same kind of pressure she had been under from the women's husbands. To her surprise, no one mentioned or even hinted about Ben Roman's treasure. Last-minute news of Steve's release had upset their plans, she supposed. Or perhaps, knowing that their overeager husbands had got nowhere, they had decided on a friendlier, more patient strategy.

Steve climbed out of the big tin bathtub, dried himself on the thin hotel towel, got into underwear and trousers. He swung open the bathroom door just in time to see Wiggins enter the hall from Susan's room, close the door quietly, and insert the key in the lock.

Steve strode into the hall. Wiggins reared around in a panic. For an instant he seemed on the verge of fleeing. Then he grinned sheepishly.

"Glad to see you been let out free, Major."

"What were you doing there?"

"Come to see Mrs. Allison. She ain't here."

"How'd you get a key?" Steve demanded.

Wiggins' mouth twitched as he tried to grin. "Most any key'll do this lock."

Steve caught the gambler's wrist and took the key from his fingers. The metal gleamed satin-bright where the collar had been filed down and where a slit had been cut into the web.

"You went to considerable trouble to get a fit," Steve said. He slipped the key into the lock, turned it and threw open the door. "Get in there."

The room was a mess. The bed had been torn up, drawers emptied. Papers were scattered everywhere. Susan's clothing was tossed helter-skelter.

Steve caught Wiggins by the lapels and backed him against the wall. He longed to beat the man within an inch of his life.

"I done it," Wiggins admitted. "I figured she might have a map with the treasure marked on it, or maybe some wrote-down directions. You and I have got to get that treasure quick, Major. Otherwise, we're going to lose it."

Steve released his hold and backed away in disgust.

"You got to listen!" Wiggins pleaded. "They've dug the whole bottom out of that cabin."

"Who has?"

"I don't know who. Some hard-faced young sprout. Last night another feller helped him. Couldn't see him plain. They worked a good part of the night."

Briefly, Steve shared Wiggins' alarm. Susan had said the treasure wouldn't be easy to find. Still, no matter how cleverly it was hidden, a determined search plus a touch of luck would unearth it.

"That ain't all," Wiggins said, "The sheriff was down there yesterday. If they trace him back, they'll find that dug-up cabin. Everybody in town'll know where the treasure is at."

"Illingsley was at the cabin?"

Wiggins nodded soberly. "The young sprout come out

and rode off. The sheriff come down off the spur and had a look inside. Then he started off after the youngster.''

"You know where they went."

"Off towards the Blacktails is all I know.''

Illingsley must have been killed shortly after that, Steve thought. But he couldn't tell Birk this without calling attention to the cabin.

"If I knowed where the treasure is at, I could sneak over and get it,'' Wiggins said. "They leave the place sometimes.''

Steve surveyed the disorder of the room. "You find anything here?''

"Nothing. You can search me." Wiggins raised his arms.

"I'm keeping you here till Susan gets back. If she finds anything missing, you're going to need a doctor.''

Steve motioned toward the connecting door and they went into his room. Wiggins sat down in a chair and propped his feet up on the bed.

"You were here in the wild days," Steve said. He took a clean shirt from a drawer and busied himself inserting cuff links. "Did you know Luke Lumby?''

"Can't say I did. Never had any hanker to know him, not that one.''

"You knew him by sight, didn't you?''

"You might say that.''

"What did he look like?''

"Well"—Wiggins' eyes narrowed as he searched his memory—"he was a short-poured man, it seems like. Not more'n five and a half feet, maybe less. Dapper dressed. Wore a mustache and beard trimmed to a point.''

"How old was he?''

Wiggins considered this a moment. "I don't remember

118

too clear. You play cards around the country, you see a lot of faces. You get mixed up."

Steve beat up a lather in a shaving mug and spread it on his face. He hung a strop over the bedpost and sharpened his razor.

"There's something else I want to know," he said, "and I want a careful answer. I want you to tell me about Susan's husband."

"I remember *him* well enough. He was a friendly, happy-spoken man that folks liked. He was what you might call active. When the mood took him, he was like as not to go out and shovel muck with the miners."

"That's Ben Roman," Steve said. "I mean her present husband—Allison."

Wiggins' glance flicked Steve and his manner immediately became guarded. "I better not say about that. I promised her not to."

"You know the man?" Steve persisted.

"I promised her not to discuss nothing whatever about him or her son."

Steve turned to his mirror and began to shave, giving no indication of his surprise. Susan had never mentioned being a mother—usually the first thing a mother tells you. He had taken it for granted she was childless.

"Can't see why she's so mysterious," he said.

"Scared of blackmail."

Steve failed to control the eager sharpness of his straight edge and nicked his chin.

"She never should've included you in with us," Wiggins said with a sudden spilling-over of resentment. "You ain't done a single blessed thing except get yourself jailed. Now you're trying to find out about her so you can blackmail her."

# THIRTEEN

Susan angrily scanned the litter of her room as Steve explained what had happened. She faced Wiggins haughtily, hating the hint of insolence in his face. She removed her hat and took a small satisfaction from his altered expression when, momentarily and quite casually, she held the hatpin in a threatening position.

"He was looking for a map or some other clue that would lead him to the money," Steve said.

"He didn't find one," Susan said icily, "because no such thing exists. But it's obvious that he's completely treacherous. I'm beginning to think that he must have conspired with Anne Barabee from the beginning."

"That ain't so," Wiggins avoided her accusing eyes and turned appealingly to Steve.

"He seemed really upset about her buying that cabin, and he had me fooled," Susan went on. "But how could she possibly have learned I wanted it except from him?"

"Now you listen to me," Wiggins said. "I never spoke

to Anne Barabee in my life except to raise my hat in the street.''

"I just had a talk with her," Susan said. "She knows that I'm not Mrs. Tanager. How do you explain that? Nobody in town knew it except you."

Wiggins made a helpless gesture.

"Explain it," Steve said.

"I can't. But how about that feller was on the stage with you—that Mexican? He was at the Frontier House in Ogden. He could've noticed you had separate rooms apart from each other and wasn't married."

"How do you know he was on the stage with us?" Steve demanded.

"I been dealing a little monte down on the flat. He got in the game one night. Quite a few Mexicans come down there sometimes. He mentioned being on that trip when the driver was bushwhacked."

"You speak Spanish?"

"*Poquito*. But this feller speaks English when he's of a mind to. He was drunk and jabbering like crazy—Spanish and English both."

Steve and Susan exchanged a glance, both wondering if this could be true. Wiggins seized the moment to change the subject.

"Mrs. Allison, we got to get hold of that money before the others find it. That's why I come looking for a map."

Susan again cast a glance over the wreckage of her room. "You get out of here now. If you try one more of your tricks—just one more—I'll wash my hands of you."

"Do that! I'll tell the sheriff about that cabin, and you'll never get near the treasure. I'll send a letter to Cedar Rapids with everything I know—"

Steve caught Wiggins' elbow and spun him toward the

121

door. "Back to your monte game. And if you ever do one thing to hurt Susan, you know what I'll do. Don't you?"

Wiggins' face was expressionless. Steve opened the door and shoved him into the hall. He watched till Wiggins disappeared down the stairs.

"He's right about one thing," he said to Susan. "We ought to get hold of that money before they tear down the cabin."

"Are you getting panicky, too?"

"It's plain the stuff isn't under the floor—you'd be worried sick if it were. If it were buried somewhere else on the lot, there would probably be a map. That leaves only the cabin walls for a hiding place."

Susan began to put the room in order. After a moment, she said, "Yes, but from what Ben told me, it won't be easy to find unless a person knows just where to look."

"What did he do—hollow out a log?"

"Well—well, yes, he did. Now you're getting *me* panicky."

"Susan, you're going to have to trust me sooner or later."

"It's hidden in a log," she said distantly.

"Is that all you know?"

"Ben told me exactly what he did," Susan said. Sighing, she reached a decision. She sat down and folded her hands in her lap.

"That first summer there was no water in town," she said. "It was hauled in and sold by the barrel. Ben and some others cooked up a scheme to pipe it in from springs on Sunrise Ridge. They made wooden pipe by splitting logs, hollowing them out, and pegging them back together sealed with pitch. Ben helped himself to a ten-foot length

122

of hollowed-out log, put the gold into it, and closed the ends with carefully fitted plugs.

"As I told you, he was part-owner of a claim down on the flat. His partners were building a cabin down there, and from time to time, Ben helped with the work. One Sunday when the others weren't around, he hauled the treasure log down there and put it into the wall. I'm the only person he ever told."

She got up and went back to the business of straightening up the room. Steve waited silently, sensing that he mustn't seem too eager to know the exact location of the log. After a moment, she faced him with an appeal for loyalty in her eyes.

"He used the log to piece out another in the north wall," she said. "It's the fourth log from the bottom. There's a partition inside the cabin that hides the joint."

"Sounds like we'll need an ax." Steve avoided her eyes as he tried to visualize the gold-laden log. "Maybe some wedges . . ."

"We can't very well go after it till the others give up."

"We'd better do it right away," Steve said. "If they tear the place down, there's a good chance they'll notice a log that's been split and pegged together."

"Ben said he made it look like any other log."

"Maybe. But I'm going down there and get the stuff. Just as soon as I can make preparations for getting it out of the territory."

"But Wiggins is down there." There was only a weak note of protest in her voice. "And whoever he's thrown in with."

"You're wrong about Wiggins. He's telling a halfway straight story, I think—though he means to get away with the whole of the treasure, of course."

"Steve, Anne made it plain to me that somebody put her up to buying that property, somebody she's afraid of. If it wasn't Wiggins, who could it be?"

Steve had continued to avoid her gaze. Now he met it.

"Luke Lumby?" he said softly.

Susan stared in amazement. "That isn't possible!"

"Think a minute. Who else would go to Anne for help?"

"He— he wouldn't dare come back!" Susan steadied herself against the chiffonier, still staring.

"How well did you know him, Susan?"

"Not at all. He and Ben stayed away from each other on purpose, I suppose. Luke was notorious. I knew him by sight, of course."

"Would you recognize him now—without his whiskers?"

"No, probably not." She closed her eyes, reaching back through eight years of spinning memories for a face. "All I really remember is that natty beard. But others who knew him better would surely recognize him if he came back."

"Anne would. And probably Bill Illingsley."

Susan drifted aimlessly to the foot of the bed, a hand raised to her cheek.

"Wiggins has been keeping an eye on you, waiting for you to come back here," Steve said. "Perhaps Lumby has been watching you, too."

"You're making wild guesses," Susan said.

"Right," he admitted. "All I've done is guess since the day I got on that stage with you."

He helped her tidy the room, piling things on the bed for her to put away. When they were finished, he said, "Susan, I know all about your past and nothing about your present."

"You know what you need to know about me," she said. As if to parry further talk about herself, she said, "I feel as if I know *you* very well."

"You don't."

"I know the essential things. Killing a man hardly upset you at all. You're a very hard case. You're also gentle and decent."

"You forgot something. I cheat at cards."

"That doesn't fit somehow." She frowned, then spoke with the hint of a smile. "I think you must have been very desperate that night. Or very angry."

"Or—" He was going to say "greedy," but changed his mind. "Why have you never mentioned that you have a son?" he asked abruptly.

Her shoulders slumped and something vital seemed to go out of her. "Wiggins told you?"

"He let it slip."

Steve waited, expecting some word of explanation from her, but none came. He strolled to the window and absently studied the weather-seared buildings across the street, heat vapor rising from roofs like some essential vigor slowly stolen from the town.

"What's the boy's name?" he asked.

"Earl."

"Earl Roman?" He kept his back to her.

"Allison."

"But he's Ben Roman's son?"

"Yes!" she said violently. She took a breath and got her emotions under control. "I suppose that's why I didn't want you to know about him. I was afraid you'd guess.

125

Wiggins knows, of course. Do you see now what a terrible sword he holds over me?''

Steve crossed the room toward her. She was arranging clothing in a drawer busily, a bit frantically. She said, ''Earl must never know who his father was. Never.''

''Susan, how much does your present husband know about your past?''

''That doesn't concern you, Steve.''

Touching her with just his fingertips, he turned her to face him. ''It concerns me very much.''

She tipped her chin at him. This was a mannerism of hers, a show of calm defiance. He sensed that now it might be taken for more than that. He drew her to him and kissed her lips, and she responded briefly, fervently. Then her arms were tight around him and her cheek hard against his shoulder.

''Steve, I need you. Terribly. In a purely practical way, I mean. I need your strength and your loyalty. That's all there is. Don't expect me to show my gratitude by loving you.''

''Words,'' he said. ''Need. Love. Gratitude. They're separated only by dim and wavering lines.''

She clung to him silently and ardently. But when he sought her lips again, she twisted her face away.

''That night in Ogden,'' she said. ''I knew at once that I needed you. To ask you to come with me seemed rash and improper. I decided that it must not also be immoral. I *decided*—do you understand?''

''No,'' he said stubbornly.

''It was settled then and forever. Otherwise, I couldn't have written you that note.''

She tried to draw away, but he held her tightly. ''Susan,

126

there's something between us. You know that. Something we can't ignore."

"We're going to get that money," she said crisply. "Then I'll pay you what I promised. Then we'll never see each other again."

He drew a deep breath and let her push away from him. He sauntered back to the window in a sultry haze of thoughts. "You have the way of a flirt," he said harshly. "A teaser."

She was hurt and didn't reply for a moment. When he faced her again, she said icily, "I thought we might be friends. From now on I shall be formal and distant. Is that what you mean?"

The few women in Steve's life had been uncomplicated and amenable to a direct approach. Susan was different. Her kind had to resist love in order to be conquered by it, he thought. When she was most emphatically determined that she didn't want him, she could be on the verge of giving in. Or was that merely what she wanted him to believe?

No, he decided angrily, her strategy was even more devious than that. She was dead-set on getting that treasure without unnecessary complications. Only afterward, when the uncertainty and the strain were over, might she react differently to him. That seemed to be what she was implying—subtly and intuitively and without the frailest shadow of overt commitment.

*She's trying to make sure of my loyalty*, he thought. *She's trying to tie me to her with a hope. I'm damned if I'll be trapped like that.*

He turned his back to her and entered his own room.

# FOURTEEN

The morning was overcast and cooler than most. A gusty wind churned dust from Center Street and slung it noisily against windows. Susan pressed a handkerchief to her nose as she and Steve came out of the hotel.

"Will it rain?" she asked anxiously.

She was wearing a simple gray serge dress and had a scarf tied over her hair. Steve carried a blanket roll under one arm. He studied the dark sky beyond the Blacktails and decided he didn't know this climate well enough to make predictions.

"If we get a gully-washer, I may need another day," he said.

"I'd understand that better if I knew what your plans are," Susan said, her tone chiding him mildly.

They bowed their heads against a fresh gust, and he took her elbow to guide her. She leaned heavily against him, and he slipped his arm around her. Even that small intimacy excited him; then he was secretly irritated with her. *Still baiting the trap*, he thought.

He said, "You're not to worry. Just do a good job of decoying."

"You have a gun on your hip this morning," she said. "I don't like that. And you haven't explained why you're carrying a blanket roll. How can I help but worry?"

"I may not be back tonight. You're not to be alarmed if I'm not."

He let go of her to clutch at his hat, making an opportunity to look over his shoulder. One of Birk's deputies had come out of the hotel and was following them. They reached the livery barn and entered its cool fragrance through a door propped open against the wind. Steve glanced back again and saw that the deputy was returning to the hotel hitchrack, where he had a mule tied.

They ordered a buggy from the liveryman, who threw a harness on a horse and led the animal around to the wagon shed. Steve helped Susan into the buggy while the horse was being hitched.

"Remember," he whispered. "Drive straight up the gulch. Keep away from Fan-tan Flat."

"Steve, will you be careful?"

"Always," he said.

"I want that treasure," she said. "But I want you back safely, too."

"Nice of you," he said lightly. He squeezed her hand and said, "Good luck."

She smiled, looking a little frightened, and drove off. Steve waved, thinking those would be the last words he ever spoke to her.

He gave the liveryman a cigar and made lighting-up an excuse to linger inside the shed.

"Will it rain?" Steve asked.

The liveryman nodded, then replied cautiously, "If it don't blow over."

Steve watched the buggy roll down Center Street and swing up the gulch road. A moment later the deputy passed the barn on his mule, the animal balky in the wind. The ruse had worked: the man had assumed that both Steve and Susan were in the buggy, and he was following it.

"I'll want a horse," Steve said.

The liveryman glanced at Steve's blanket roll. "For how long?"

"I'll have him back by dark."

Five minutes later, he led a long-barreled bay out the back door of the barn and mounted. The sky had darkened a bit, he judged, and the wind had taken on a sharp coolness. His guess was that the first rain clouds might blow over but that he was pretty sure to get wet before the day was over. Keeping to alleys and back streets, he rode southeast through the town and headed into rolling country in search of a way up Sunrise Ridge that wouldn't take him squarely into the field of Tim Gaul's telescope.

The bay was nervous and kept trying to veer back toward town. Skirting a steep slope, Steve found himself in view of Tim's cabin after all. He could only hope that the old vigilante had his glass pointed somewhere else—at Susan's buggy, maybe.

In a little more than an hour, he reached the Gill ranch, where he had learned there were horses for sale. He found Ab Gill a pale-eyed, tobacco-stained man eager to haggle. When the bargaining was over, Steve owned two tough-looking cow ponies and a saddle. Gill threw in a bridle and lead rope. Steve took his noon meal at the ranch and seized the opportunity of asking questions about the surrounding country.

By early afternoon, he was on his way, circling northwest. He was perhaps being more circuitous than he needed to be, he thought, but he wanted no unnecessary risks at this stage of the game. He could have bought horses at the livery, of course; but the news would have been all over town in no time and would very likely have put a deputy on his trail. Moreover, he didn't want Susan to know about the horses. The purchase of two of them would make it pretty plain that he was planning to ride out of the territory.

Lightning veined the black sky ahead, and thunder rolled ominously close. The horses he was leading kept trotting up past him, making themselves hard to handle. He decided to take shelter in a little cluster of cottonwoods near the base of a hill, and he reached it just as the first huge raindrops splashed down on him. Lightning crashed blindingly close, terrifying the horses. Steve quieted the animals, donned his slicker, and stayed mounted in order to keep his saddle dry.

The rain came in sheets. The horses turned their rumps to the wind and quieted down. In a quarter of an hour the downpour slacked up enough so that he could again be on his way.

The sun stabbed through broken clouds as he reached the stage road where it looped around the Blacktails and entered Star Gulch. He took the road up-gulch till he guessed he was close to Fan-tan Flat; then he worked his way into the hills to the west in search of a place to hide his extra horses. He tethered them in a steep-sided little ravine where there was good browse, then prodded the livery horse on through hilly country till he struck the upper point of the flat.

He rode close to the treasure cabin and saw that boards and stovepipe had been piled beside the door. A soggy straw tick lay a few yards away. He rode on to Wiggins' cabin and dismounted. Wiggins came to the door staring and disheveled, as if he had been asleep.

"Nobody seen you come here?" he demanded.

"Let's hope not." Steve pushed past him into the dingy interior. Blankets lay on a pile of hay in a corner. The only furniture was a table and a pair of benches. The table held a candle and a pack of playing cards.

"Make yourself to home," Wiggins said. "It ain't what you'd call fancy, but I only paid five dollars for a month's rent."

"What's new next door?" Steve jerked his head in the direction of the other cabin.

"The young feller was there a while this morning. Rode off before the rain. We going after the money now?"

"I'm going over there for a look," Steve said, shedding the slicker. "You wait here."

He walked the hundred yards stiffly, breathing the wet fragrance of sagebrush and weighing the news that the cabin was unoccupied. He had planned on making a prisoner of the treasure-digger.

The entire floor of the cabin had been excavated and partly filled in. Some of the dirt had been pitched through the door and window; some of it had been thrown behind the digger as he abandoned sections of his pit. The result was a hummocky underfooting of soft earth.

The partition that divided the cabin had been torn away, all but its top log. This made it easier to spot the ten-foot length of log in the northeast corner of the cabin, exactly where Susan said it would be. Steve made his way to it for a closer inspection. If there was a pegged seam in it, this was covered by the logs above and below, or by the clay chinking. Except that its corner end had been less deeply notched, there was nothing to distinguish this log from any other. .

He returned to Wiggins' cabin, drew an envelope and stub of pencil from his pockets, and began to prepare a list.

"Go up to the town and buy these things for me," he said. "They're things I couldn't get without causing a good deal of curiosity." He passed the list to Wiggins and explained each item. "A small saw. A keyhole or compass saw, something with a narrow blade . . . An ax. Single-bitted, so I can use it for a sledge as well . . . Two wedges I can use to split a log. Get single-bitted axheads if you can't find anything else . . . A pair of saddlebags. The biggest you can find . . . A canteen . . . Five pounds of jerky and a tin of hardtack . . . You keep a horse down here?"

Wiggins grunted affirmatively. "He's in a shed down by the road."

"All right, you lead mine back to the livery. Tell the stableman I asked you to return it for me. Don't mention where I am. You got all that straight?"

Wiggins was studying the list, gaping at it. "Looks like that treasure might be in the cabin wall."

"Don't think!" Steve snapped. "Just get that stuff and get back here. For once in your life, don't fritz things up. Try one of your stupid tricks and you could wind up dead."

Wiggins sensed that he was a vital cog in Steve's plans and could afford to take offense. He said petulantly, "I'm tired of your damn threats."

133

"I'm tired of them, too," Steve said. "Cross me now, and there'll be no threat, no warning. Do you understand that?"

Something in the snow-soft voice prompted Wiggins to hold his tongue, even to nod faintly. He tucked his great thatch of hair in and around his derby and was on his way. Steve stood in the doorway and watched him jog toward the road. In the lower part of the flat, the Chinese had come out of their buildings after the rain and gone back to work, unheeding, antlike figures in the distance.

Deputy Riggs McClean stood in the sheriff's office and gestured helplessly. His profanity had the ring of a hammer on an anvil.

"How in the screamin' tarnation could I know she was alone in that buggy?" he demanded. "They went into the wagon shed. The buggy rolled out and headed up the gulch. How could I—"

"You couldn't," Smiley Birk said, elevating his feet to his desk and crossing them. "I'd have done the exact same thing you did—and looked just as big a souphead. One man can't watch two people when they go off in different directions, and I can't spare another deputy. Where's Mrs. Tanager now?"

"Back at the hotel."

"You better get back there. She may have some plan to sneak off and join the major. The judge chewed me up one side and down the other for letting him out of jail. If they get that treasure without our knowing it, the old boy will have a stroke."

"Maybe Tim Gaul got his spyglass on Tanager," McClean said hopefully.

"Maybe. If Tim hasn't gone out-and-out loco after trying to call that meeting last night."

"I hadn't heard," McClean said.

"He went around notifying all the old vigilantes to meet at the Masonic Hall. They're all pretty upset about Illingsley, and if they didn't all know that Tim has slipped a buckle, something might've come of it. As it was, nobody showed up but Tim."

McClean wagged his head sadly as he turned to go back to his post. "Must've jarred the old boy."

"He's been jarred too damn much lately," Birk said. "I don't like it a bit."


Susan ate a late lunch and went at once to her room. She rearranged the pillows on her bed and settled down with a volume of Emerson's *Essays*, determined to face the wait ahead of her in a relaxed manner. She opened the book to "Self-Reliance." This was ironic, she thought, when at this moment in her life she was relying completely on someone else. Steve had told her little of his plans. All she could be really sure of was that he meant to get the treasure. She prayed he wouldn't have to kill again. Or be killed—she wouldn't even think of that.

She trusted him completely, she assured herself. She hadn't really intended to, but—well, he was certainly highly capable of meeting the situation that had developed. *And he wouldn't cheat me*, she thought. *We've become friends. He cares about me . . .*

She turned the pages to "Circles" and tried to lose herself in the niceties of Emerson's metaphysics. But the storm bombarded the town now. Thunder shook the hotel like a rickety toy. Lightning kindled an uneasiness in her that had nothing to do with fear of being struck. The storm seemed to be in some weird way an echo of turmoil in the remote reaches of her being. A single sentence leaped at her from the page, and she read it aloud: "The sweet of nature is love; yet if I have a friend, I am tormented by my imperfection."

She laid aside the book to ponder the words. Then, forcing herself to stay quietly on the bed, she sought to find in them a guide to practical action. She would do exactly what she had told Steve she would do, she decided. When they got to Ogden with the money, she would pay him what she had promised. Well, perhaps she would give him a small bonus. Then she would never see him again . . .

Rain washed the windows and wind rattled them. Soon the thunder faded to a grumble, and Susan drifted into lassitude. She slept, long and heavily. She woke to a determined rapping and was amazed to see sunshine pouring through the west window. She got up and opened the door, and the desk clerk handed her a note.

"A kid brought it," he said.

It was in a plain envelope, lightly sealed. Susan felt a twinge of disappointment when she saw the neat feminine handwriting; she had hoped at first—ridiculously—that the message was from Steve. She read it quickly.

DEAR SUE:

I would like to explain everything, but I don't dare visit you. Could you please come to my shop about seven-thirty?

ANNE

She got her purse from a drawer and consulted the small gold watch that she kept in it. She was surprised that she had slept so long; it was after five. Anne was a little late with an offer of explanations, she thought; but she knew she would keep the appointment. Her curiosity would nag her into it even though Anne deserved to be ignored. And it would be nice to have something to do besides waiting with a volume of Emerson.

# FIFTEEN

Slim Wiggins rode the livery horse and led his own. He rode at a walk. A man couldn't think at a trot.

The major knew where the treasure was—that was plain as the ace of spades. He meant to get it right away. This was the day Wiggins had been dreaming about for eight years. But unless he did something pretty decisive, it wasn't going to be much like the dream.

The major had another horse hidden someplace near the flat, he decided. Otherwise, returning this one didn't make sense. And what about the list Wiggins had in his pocket? Saddlebags. Hardtack and jerky. And what about the blanket roll the major was packing? The only possible conclusion was that the major was going to hopskotch right out of the territory as soon as he got the money.

He might or might not be double-dealing Mrs. Allison. They might have agreed to meet someplace. In that case, Wiggins could follow her to Iowa and blackmail her out of most everything. But he couldn't count on their meeting

He had to play it as if he would never get another chance at the money after tonight.

"I got to kill him now," Wiggins uttered. "I got to be almighty careful about it."

He was, he admitted, scared sick of the major. Of the man himself, but especially of the man's luck. Luck was Wiggins' great enemy. He had devoted his life to perfecting skills calculated to eliminate it from various card games, yet it was always bobbing up to ruin him. Like a few weeks ago in Cheyenne when he had dealt himself a king full and got beaten out of a two-hundred-dollar pot by a drunken cowhand with a perfectly honest four treys. You couldn't beat a man when his luck was right. And in the matter of staying alive, the major was riding a streak. Oh, he was wolf smart, all right, and pit-dog tough; but it was obscene, uncanny, capital luck that had kept him alive.

This, Wiggins believed with all his heart, and he felt a crushing dread of the task before him.

"I got to *kill* him tonight," he told himself again. "I got to do it in a way that eliminates luck out of the picture."

He turned up Sunrise Gulch and entered the town. As he approached the livery, a woman drove a one-horse wagon away from it. She was Anne Barabee. He watched her drive up a side street and into an alley toward the back of her shop. Trying to sound as if he were just making conversation, he asked the liveryman what a dressmaker wanted with a wagon.

"Said she had some movin' to do." The man gave Wiggins a wink. "I offered to help. She said no."

Susan had supper in the hotel dining room, eating leisurely and managing to finish at exactly seven-thirty by

139

the watch in her purse. Arranging a scarf over her head, she left by the street door and crossed toward Anne's shop.

The mountain air was winey after the storm. A smear of black clouds beyond the Blacktails had spoiled the sunset and suggested that more rain was on its way. Susan hoped Steve wouldn't get caught in it.

As she reached for the latch on Anne's door, it swung open. Anne faced her with a shaky smile and stepped back to make way for her. Susan sensed at once that something was wrong. The curtains had been drawn and the room was half-dark. She almost collided with the big table in the center of the room. She heard the door close behind her and the bolt clank into place.

"I'm sorry," Anne said immediately. "I've brought you here under false pretenses."

"What on earth do you mean?"

"Sit down," Anne said.

Susan uneasily made her way toward a chair near the curtained doorway to the back room. To reach it, she had to edge around a large trunk that sat between the table and the wall. She perched tensely on the edge of the chair.

"Anne," she said, "you're being awfully mysterious. I wish—"

The curtain in the doorway billowed outward and a man swaggered into the room.

"This is Ernie Smith," Anne said tonelessly.

Susan found herself on her feet, staring in exasperation at first one and then the other. A grin creased Ernie Smith's insolent young face as he stepped close to her, one hand on the butt of the low-slung revolver he wore.

"We want you to tell us exactly where the treasure is hidden," Anne said.

"Exactly," Ernie Smith said.

Susan started toward the door, but he blocked her way. He still had his right hand on the holstered gun. Steve had snatched a gun from that holster, she thought; Ernie was surely taking no chances of that ever happening again. She was suddenly less afraid of him.

"And if I don't choose to tell you?" she said.

"We won't talk about that," Anne said, "because you're going to. You really have nothing to lose, Sue. We have the property, so we're bound to find the treasure eventually. It's just that we're in a hurry."

Susan attempted to stand up again. Ernie's hand on her shoulder kept her in the chair. Ernie grinned down at her.

"I'll tell the authorities first," Susan said. "I'll let them confiscate the money."

For an instant, Anne looked genuinely distressed. "We're not going to let you do that."

"I'm sure a deputy followed me here," Susan said. "He follows me everywhere. Now I'd like to leave, please. If you try to stop me, I'll—I'll scream."

"Sue, I hope you understand that I have to do this," Anne said. "I've been forced into it. I suddenly have a chance to get away from this country forever, to have a decent, comfortable life—"

"Decent?" Susan snapped. "With Luke Lumby?"

Anne was shaken, but she kept her voice calm. "So you've guessed. It's just as well. You can understand that we intend to hold you till you tell us where the treasure is. We've made arrangements to take you to a much safer place."

"I guess there's nothing else to do," Susan said. She took a deep breath and opened her mouth to scream. Ernie was ready for her. His rough hand clamped her mouth before she had fairly started. She managed to bite a finger.

His open-handed blow sent blinding lights through her brain and knocked her off the chair.

She was lying prone then, and someone was holding her scarf over her mouth. Someone else was sitting on her legs and tying her hands behind her, then her ankles. The scarf was forced into her mouth and cruelly bound into place with a bandanna. Another bandanna was tied over her eyes.

"We'll wait for it to get a little darker before we move out," a soft masculine voice said. "Just a few minutes."

Susan realized that a second man had come into the room. *Luke Lumby*, she thought. *He was waiting in the back.* The strange thing was that his voice seemed vaguely familiar.

"What are you doing?" he intoned softly.

"Punching air holes in the trunk," Anne said. "We don't want her to smother."


Having posted himself in the lobby where he had a view into the dining room, Deputy Riggs McClean saw Susan leave by the street door. From the main doorway, he watched her pick her way across the muddy street and enter the dressmaker's shop. She was making a social visit, he supposed. From what he'd heard, both she and Anne Barabee had been outlaws' women. No doubt they had a lot to talk about.

More to kill time than anything else, Riggs crossed the street and strolled past the shop, hearing indistinct voices inside. A sound that might have been a choked-off scream brought him to a stop; then he walked on. Women were always squealing or screaming or making noises somewhere in between. It meant they were having a good time.

He recrossed the street to the hardware store. Lige Peckinpaw, a leading member of the town's spit-and-whittle set, lounged alone on a bench against the façade. Both men nodded without speaking. Lige fired a stream of tobacco juice across the boardwalk and a full ten feet into the street.

"What's goin' on over there?" Lige said as the deputy eased down beside him. "The Barabee woman movin'?"

"Movin'?" Riggs said, "I hadn't heard."

"She's got a spring wagon in back. Driv it up herself."

"I'll be damned," Riggs said without enthusiasm. He shaped up a cigarette and got it going.

"Couple of saddlehorses out in back, too."

"Whose?"

"Dang if I know," Lige said.

Riggs sat and smoked as darkness crept into the town. Lights began to fill windows, but none appeared behind the thin curtains of the dressmaking shop. There were a few feet of space between the shop and the next building, and Riggs saw a light flare briefly in the alley. Definite sounds of activity came from back of the shop—muffled voices, the thud and scrape of something being loaded into a wagon.

"Guess I'll have a look," Riggs said.

He crossed the street and sauntered between the buildings to the alley, reaching it just as the wagon began to pull away. There were two figures on the seat, their backs toward him. Someone else held two saddlehorses to one side of the alley as the wagon passed.

"Hold up there!" Riggs called. "Deputy sheriff here."

The occupants of the wagon seat turned around in surprise. Riggs recognized. Anne Barabee beside the man who was driving. The wagon rumbled to a stop a few yards beyond the saddlehorses.

Riggs strode forward, supposing he was making a fool of himself by sticking his nose into some innocent errand. He gave a glance to the man holding the horses and didn't recognize him. A step later, the toe of a boot struck Riggs in the angle behind his knee, bearing down with a man's full weight on it. Riggs crashed forward to his hands and knees. Something knocked his hat off. Then a revolver barrel chopped viciously at the base of his skull.

He came to slowly, resisting consciousness and the sickening pain it brought. He was a long time getting to his feet; then it took a minute to figure out where he was. At last, he made his way to Center Street and careened across it. The hardware store was dark. Lige Peckinpaw was no longer on the bench. Riggs made out the looming hulk of the courthouse half a block away and knew he couldn't make it. Then he collided with someone and was shoved against the storefront.

"You drunk on duty?" Tim Gaul demanded.

"Tim, I been slugged," Riggs said. "Give me a hand to the office."

# SIXTEEN

The lower end of Fan-tan Flat was a sluice-tangled confusion of black buildings seeping wannish light. Wiggins reined to the shack he used as a stable, deciding to leave his horse there and let it fill up on hay. If things worked out, he would be riding hard and far tonight.

He unfastened the bulging gunny sack slung to his saddlehorn and dismounted. It had taken time, but he had scared up all the items on the list. And he had bought one that wasn't on it—a snub little .38 revolver that was tucked under his belt, concealed by his coat. With the sack over his shoulder, he trudged to his cabin.

Steve had got a fire going in the blackened, crumbling fireplace and had coffee heating. He took the sack from Wiggins and emptied it on the floor. Wiggins took advantage of the moment to shed his coat, slipping the revolver into a pocket. He hung the garment on a peg near the door and folded the sagging pocket out of sight against the wall.

Steve was sorting out the tools and supplies. He said, "Looks like you got it all."

"We going to work now?" Wiggins asked eagerly.

"We'll eat first. Don't you keep any grub except coffee?"

"Too many rats," Wiggins said. "I eat out."

They sipped stout black coffee and munched the hardtack and jerky Wiggins had brought from town. When they had finished, Steve packed the remainder of the food into his blanket roll. He picked up the large horsehide saddlebags Wiggins had brought and examined them with satisfaction.

"Somebody coming," Wiggins said.

They stood motionless, listening to the chop of hoofs approaching across the flat. Wiggins stepped to the door and eased it open. Steve snuffed the candle and joined him. After a moment, three horsemen trotted up to the cabin.

"Birk!" Steve whispered, drawing Wiggins away from the door. "I'll keep out of sight. You get rid of him."

"Anybody in there?" Birk called.

Wiggins gave the sheriff a moment to dismount, then jerked the door wide.

"What you want?"

"Who's in there with you?" Birk demanded.

"Nobody."

"We heard Major Tanager was down here."

Tim Gaul and his damned telescope, Steve thought. The old vigilante had spotted his arrival here and had identified him.

"I guess I know who you mean," Wiggins said. "Big feller. He was riding a livery horse, asked me to take it back for him. When I got back here he was gone. Must've had another horse somewheres close by."

"That'll be him," Birk said, apparently convinced. To

the men with him, he said, "We'll have a look at that other cabin."

That wouldn't do, Steve thought. One look at that dug-up floor and Birk would guess that the treasure hunt centered there. Likely as not, he would put the place under guard.

"Wait!" Steve called. "You looking for me, Smiley?"

Birk's profanity rang through the cabin as he pushed past Wiggins. "You're jumping damn right I am! What's going on, Tanager? Who slugged my deputy and where in hell is your wife?"

"Probably at the hotel." Steve scraped a match across the tabletop and held it to the candle. "I wouldn't know about the deputy."

Birk stopped short, appraising Steve in the shifting light. The two deputies drifted into the cabin and stood behind the sheriff.

"She isn't at the hotel." Birk spoke grimly and paused to study the effect of this announcement. "She went to Anne Barabee's shop. Riggs McClean saw Anne Barabee and two men leaving from in back of the place. They had a wagon with a trunk in it. Riggs started to nose around and got himself gun-barreled."

Steve understood then, and understanding was like a sudden sickness. He placed a hand on the table to steady himself.

"Smiley," he said, "you sure she's nowhere in town?"

Birk shook his head. "Near as I can figure it, she was in that trunk."

Steve felt the need of violent words but could find none violent enough. He stood braced against the table, staring down at it, shaking his head helplessly. Yes, they would take her out of town. But where? To one of the dozen abandoned cabins in these hills? To some crumbling mineshaft? To a camp buried in some lonely, brush-choked gulch?

"I figured it might be something you'd planned—a scheme to sneak her out of town," Birk said. A softness came into his voice. "I guess it wasn't."

"They mean to make her tell where the treasure is," Steve said.

"Who, Major?"

"Guesses won't help. The important thing is *where*."

"The wagon was seen turning down-gulch," Birk said. "I thought— Hell, it must've gone on down the road. You riding with us?"

"You get going. My horse is staked out. I'll be along as soon as I saddle up."

Birk gave him a sharp look, then nodded and wheeled out of the cabin. The deputies followed.

"You ain't really going with 'em?" Wiggins said.

"No."

"Whoever's got her will make her talk. They'll be down here, Major. We got to hurry, Major. Now or never, as the feller says."

*Now or never*, Steve thought. He stooped to gather up the tools that lay scattered on the floor. *There's nothing I can do for her now that Birk can't do as well—better, maybe; he knows the country. Forget her. Get the money. Get out*.

He put the axheads Wiggins had brought to be used as wedges into one of the saddlebags and slung them over his shoulder; then he picked up the bed roll and canteen. He paused to face Wiggins, looking him over and deciding he wasn't armed.

148

"Now listen carefully," Steve said. "The treasure is in a ten-foot log in the north wall. I won't need your help to get it. You keep watch—a damned close watch."

Wiggins nodded agreeably. "I'll post myself on guard at the west end of the cabin. That digging feller always comes from the west."

*From the west*, Steve thought. *That's the way I came—south parallel to the buttes, then west across the flat. And I didn't see a single cabin or mine over that way.*

"You said Illingsley rode off that way, too," Steve said. "The day he was killed."

"That's right. He was tailing the digging feller." Wiggins moved past Steve and laid a hand on his coat, not taking it from the peg. Steve paid him no attention.

"You suppose they've got a camp—" Steve broke off. "Bring the ax and the candle," he said.

He strode into the darkness toward the other cabin. Damn damnation! What had Tim Gaul said about a cabin pinched into a patch of pine part-way up the north butte? Road Agents' Roost, Tim had called it. He had described in detail how he found the trail leading up to it. Hidden behind a boulder on the edge of a draw thick with chokeberry, he had said . . .

*I could never find it in the dark*, Steve told himself. Yet he knew there might be a chance if he scouted straight along the foot of the butte.

He made himself stop thinking about it. The treasure lay only a few yards away in a log he could roll out of the wall and split in maybe half an hour. And the hell with your lofty list of things money wouldn't buy. It would buy a business or a ranch, a life worth living for its own sake. It would buy freedom from the shallow substitute that was the Game.

149

Rain suddenly began to fall, and he bent into an easy run. If the rain kept up, he thought, it would hide his trail. With two horses to carry him and the money, he ought to be in Fort Benton in three days—perhaps less if he could do some horse-trading along the way. At Benton, if he was lucky, he might catch a paddle-wheeler going down the Missouri. More likely he would buy a new outfit and go overland to Bismarck, where the N.P. railhead was . . .

Wiggins had put on his coat and was following at a distance of half a dozen yards. He carried the ax and candle in his left hand. His right gripped the revolver in his pocket.

*Now*, he kept telling himself. *Now*. The major's arms were full. His back was turned. He had told where the treasure was. It was time for him to die.

Wiggins drew the gun, trembling, shoving it back into his pocket when the rain came and the major began to run. Wiggins ran, too, closing the distance between them a little. When the major reached the doorway, Wiggins drew the gun again, cocked it, and fired, knowing that he wouldn't miss.

The blow of the bullet plunged Steve into the dark interior of the cabin. He lost his footing on the uneven floor and half-fell, half-dived into soft and fragrant earth. He rolled, shedding the saddlebags, surprised to find his own gun solidly in his hand.

Wiggins fired again, sending the shot low into the blackness of the doorway. Thanks to the dug-up floor, Steve lay below the level of the threshold, and the bullet missed. Wiggins advanced, peering warily, muttering something. Steve thumbed two quick shots, saw Wiggins go limp, saw him spin headlong into the night.

Steve leaped to his feet, wondering that he could move

at all. Wiggins lay face-down a few steps beyond the door. Steve found the man's weapon and flung it away. He tore off his own coat then, bewildered by the absence of weakness and pain after the jarring blow he had felt in his back. There was no blood on the coat, no hole in it. Numbly, he realized that Wiggins' bullet had struck the saddlebag that had hung behind his left shoulder—the bag with the axheads in it.

Wiggins pulled himself to his hands and knees and began to whine softly. Still holding his gun, Steve was tempted to fire again, but he lowered the weapon and eased down the hammer. He couldn't dispatch a wounded man as he might a wounded animal.

He half-carried Wiggins into the cabin, lighted the candle, and stripped him to the waist. Wiggins moaned in pale and wide-eyed terror.

"I'm scared to die. I'm too wicked to die."

One bullet had torn into his right shoulder, smashing the collarbone and going on through. The other was lower. It might have nicked a lung, Steve thought.

"You might have a chance if I can stop the bleeding," he said. He tore bandages from those parts of Wiggins' shirt and undershirt that were not blood-soaked, and he bound the wounds as tightly as he could.

"I got to have a doctor," Wiggins whined. "A man of God to save my soul from Hell."

"Shut up," Steve said. "Save your strength."

Wiggins seemed not to hear him. "I'm scared to die. I never believed in Hell. Now I do and I'm scared."

Steve made a trip to the other cabin for blankets and made the man as comfortable as he could. Wiggins had taken a chill; through chattering teeth, he still gasped his terror of death.

"Shut up!" Steve bellowed at him. "Lie quiet and try not to snivel yourself to death. I've got work to do. After that, I'll send a Chinese for a doctor."

Steve carried the tools to the far end of the cabin, adding the pick and shovel left by the unknown digger. The top log of the partition had not been removed, he noticed. It seemed a superfluous, vaguely threatening beam, and he struck it with the shovel to make sure it was solidly fastened.

He leveled a place near the north wall and arranged some loose boards to improve his footing. Using the pickend, he scraped clay chinking from above and below the treasure log. Then he attacked it with the knife-bladed compass saw, cutting into the notched end at the corner of the cabin. This was tedious work, but it was the only way he could think of to free the length of log from the wall.

*Road Agents' Roost.* The trunk-laden wagon had headed down-gulch, Birk had said—and the stage road curled close to the north butte . . . The more he thought about it, the more certain Steve was that Susan had been taken up there. And the certainty tormented him.

She would be stubborn about co-operating with them; somehow he was sure of that. What blunt, brutal torture would they apply to make her talk? And when she had talked, would they kill her? He assured himself they wouldn't.

He swore at the toughness of the log and drove the saw faster. His arm ached from sawing. Off to his left, Wiggins dismally intoned his fear of death.

You couldn't blame him too much, Steve thought. He had seen better men than Wiggins die afraid.

And women? How did women die?

The saw screeched into a knot and buckled. He wretched it from the cut and flung it to the ground.

He was running across the flat then, cursing the rain and his heavy boots, cursing himself for picketing the horses so far away. Minutes later he was in the saddle, defying rough country, rain, and starless night by pushing his horse into a lope.

The butte itself was invisible until he reached its benchlike shoulder. Riding along this, he came almost at once to the draw Tim Gaul had mentioned; then he lost long minutes looking for the boulder that marked the foot of the trail. He found it finally, smaller than he had expected and screened by brush.

Judging it impossible to find his way on horseback in the dark, he started up afoot, leading his horse. All tracks had been washed out—if there had ever been any. In places, water rushing from the wall of the butte had washed away the trail itself. There was nothing to confirm his judgment that Susan and her captors were somewhere on the great black wall above him. Frustration hammered at him; he was quite possibly chasing the wildest of geese. Then he rounded a fortress-like outcropping into a shallow cavity and came upon the horses—three of them.

He scrambled up the rest of the way without regard for his wind or pounding heart, and he was gasping when he reached the pines. He wound slowly through them and almost walked into the cabin wall before he saw it. He stood motionless and after a moment was rewarded by the sound of voices—a man's and a woman's. Rounding a corner of the building, he made out frail flecks of light that seeped from a curtained window; a sharp luminous line marked the bottom of the cabin door. He filled his lungs with pine-sweetened air and paused to think.

He had no plan. He inclination was to draw his gun and plunge inside; but he rejected rashness now. Better to wait, listen, choose his moment. He turned, thinking to post himself at a corner of the cabin, and he found himself face to face with a grinning man and a cocked revolver.

"Evening, Major," Ernie Smith said scarcely two yards away. "I been right behind you since you topped the trail. A man walks silent on this duff."

# SEVENTEEN

Susan lay twisted in the trunk and thought that this was
what death might be like: smothered existence in a space-
less black hell with an overwhelming wish for freedom
eternally denied. For a time she surrendered to the jolting
darkness. She grew drowsy; then, panicked by the thought
she might be suffocating, she began to work the gag out of
her mouth. By elaborate facial contortions and by rubbing
her cheek against the side of the trunk, she managed it.

She thought of screaming, but that seemed useless now.
She was being taken out of town, she supposed, to some
remote place where Anne and her cutthroat friends meant
to tear the truth from her. The thought came to her that
they might be taking her to the treasure cabin, and hope
flared briefly—Steve might be there. Then she realized
that Fan-tan Flat would not be remote enough; odd doings
there might be noticed by some of the Chinese, who might
investigate.

She had the black thought then that Steve was dead, that

Anne's friends had been at the cabin when he arrived and that they had killed him. But she rejected that; she had to reject it or give in to the creeping numbness that racked her and die. Not Steve. He had worn a gun this morning. He would have wounded one of them at the very least . . .

The wagon stopped. After a moment someone lifted the lid of the trunk. Still blindfolded, Susan tasted the freshness of the night air and blessed it. Masculine hands pulled her to her feet and lifted her out of the trunk. She recognized the soft voice of the man she hadn't seen and Ernie Smith's drawling tenor. Someone bent beside her and slashed the rope that bound her ankles. No one seemed to notice that she was no longer gagged.

She took a deep breath and let out a scream that she hadn't known she was capable of, a scream to put a baying hound to shame, to start a landslide . . .

The blow knocked her off the end of the wagon. There was the sickening jolt of the fall; then she was lying with her cheek against the wet earth, struggling for breath.

"Easy," the soft-voiced man said. "Don't break the lady's neck before she's had a chance to talk to us."

"She won't try that again." Ernie Smith said proudly.

Shaken and breathless though she was, Susan tried it again. Fingers seized her hair, pressing her mouth into the mud.

"Stop it!" Anne Barabee said—and it came to Susan as a surprise that Anne was with them. "No one's likely to hear her."

"She's got to be gagged," the soft voice said.

"Gag her then," Anne said. "But stop acting like animals."

A handkerchief clamped Susan's mouth. She was lifted to her feet.

156

"Put her on the roan," the soft voice said.

This proved to be an awkward operation. One of the men picked her up; the other mounted the horse behind the saddle and pulled her right leg over the animal. Finally she was boosted aboard and found herself sitting a man's saddle for the first time since her childhood.

"I'll ditch the wagon where it won't be found till morning," the soft voice said. "I'll be along on the harness horse. Move off now."

It was Ernie Smith who sat behind her, his arms encircling her. Somebody handed him the reins. They rode off at a walk over hilly country. Another horse with Anne aboard followed closely.

Susan was beyond humiliation now, almost beyond fear. Curiously, she could think quite clearly and with a strange detachment. They would eventually make her tell about the treasure, of course. And if they got it, they were likely as not to kill her. All she could do was delay as long as possible, give Steve every chance to get it out of the cabin. If her captors found it gone, there might be more delay—perhaps an effort to make a deal with Steve.

They began a steep and tortuous ascent, the horse sulling and requiring all of Ernie Smith's attention. After some minutes of this, they halted. Ernie dismounted and hauled her down from the saddle. He untied her hands, removed the gag and blindfold.

They were in a strange little hollow that seemed to be on the edge of creation. The formidable wall of the butte loomed above them. In the other direction there was a black void. Anne had dismounted and now came to Susan's side. She spoke tonelessly.

"We have a climb on foot ahead. I'll go first."

Susan climbed slowly, pretending exhaustion, stopping

157

to rest every few steps. Behind her, Ernie Smith grumbled and prodded, but she delayed as much as she could. Even when rain suddenly began to fall, she continued to poke along.

They reached the cabin sopping wet. Ernie lighted a candle that rose from a mass of drippings on a plank table. He pushed Susan toward a bench at one side of the table and grunted at her to sit down. After a moment, Anne came and sat across the table from her.

"I'm sorry it has to be like this, Sue."

"You've gone out of your mind," Susan said.

"We have as much right to that money as you or anyone else! We intend to get it. Tonight."

Susan met Anne's eyes and said nothing. Ernie Smith came up behind Susan, put his hands on her shoulders and ran them down to her wrists. He pulled her hands behind her back and quickly bound them again. After that he blindfolded her with a rain-soaked bandanna.

"Be sensible, Sue," Anne said. "You can get very badly hurt if you're not."

"Myself, I hope she ain't sensible," Ernie Smith said. He pulled Susan back against his body and held her there. Gently, he stroked her throat.

"Get away from her," Anne said. Ernie took his time about it, but he obeyed. Anne said to Susan, "You have till Luke gets here to think it over. Think carefully."

It seemed a long time before Luke arrived, a time of silence with Anne moving around the cabin and Ernie going out and coming back, announcing that Luke was on his way up the trail. Luke called from outside the door, not coming in until he was assured that Susan was blindfolded. This was a good sign, she decided: if he planned to kill her, he wouldn't care if she saw his face.

158

"Is the little lady ready to co-operate?" he said. Again the voice stirred a vague response in Susan's memory.

"I think so," Anne said.

"Ernie," Luke said, "go outside. Keep a lookout."

"Why?" Ernie sounded surprised. "Who'd be comin' up here?"

"Who knows? Anne tells me the place has been discovered."

"And forgotten," Anne said.

"Get out there," Luke said to Ernie. "There's no telling how much of a war dance that deputy's stirred up. Somebody just might think of this place."

"Tim Gaul would be the only one," Anne said. "He's the one who found it. He would remember."

"That would suit me to a T," Luke said.

Ernie went out. Anne dragged out the bench across the table from Susan and sat there again. Luke moved behind Susan and put his hands on her shoulders as Ernie had done.

"Now," he said pleasantly, "are you going to tell us where the treasure is?"

Susan said nothing. Luke's fingers tightened on her shoulders.

"Sue, please—" Anne began.

"You'd better go outside," Luke said.

Anne sighed wearily. Her bench scraped back a few inches, but she didn't get up.

"If you want my co-operation, why don't you offer some yourself?" Susan said.

"What do you mean by that?" Luke said.

"I don't know how much treasure there is, but I'm sure there's a large amount. Share it with me. If you do that, naturally I won't jeopardize my share by going to the law.''

"All right," Luke said. "We'll make it worthwhile to keep your mouth shut. Now where is it?"

"I want half."

"All right, half."

The door banged open. Ernie Smith said, "Somebody working his way up the trail. One man."

"Tim Gaul!" Luke said.

"He don't move like Gaul. Looks more like Tanager. I'm pretty sure of that."

Luke moved away from Susan and began to pace the floor. Finally, he said, "Ernie, can you take him alone?"

"Easy."

"I want him alive, and I want him blindfolded before he's brought in here. Bring him to the door and make him turn his back to it. I'll cover him from the doorway while you blindfold him and tie his hands. Let him know he's covered, but he mustn't see me."

"Listen," Ernie said. "We owe him something for Danny. It sounds to me like you mean to let him off."

"When did you start making the plans?" A touch of steel crept into the soft voice.

"I didn't. Only—"

"Then until I decide exactly what we're going to do, he'll be tied and blindfolded."

"Sure," Ernie said.

Luke went out with Ernie, saying he wanted to see the approaching man for himself. Anne moaned.

"I don't like this, Sue—not a bit. But when there's a lot of money to be had, things like this happen. Nobody ever gets hold of a lot of money without hurting somebody."

Susan hardly heard her. She sat with her arms clamped

behind her, her dress wet from the rain, her body bruised and shaken by the rough treatment she had taken. Now she was overwhelmed by a strange mixture of fear and elation.

Steve had somehow learned where she was and had come after her! She had doubted him; she understood that now. She had finally let him go after the treasure in his own strange way because her nerves were frayed by the helpless waiting. But there was another reason she had scarcely been aware of. She had wanted to know if he was loyal to her. She had wanted to test him. And though she hadn't allowed the thought to crystallize till now, she had been willing to risk the treasure to make the test. And now he was scrambling up the wall of the butte toward her— and into the guns of men who had seen him coming!

"Luke and I will go to South America," Anne said. "We'll use the money for a fresh start."

The weary desperation in Anne's tone touched Susan's pity. Luke had come back for the money, not for Anne. That was a simple truth that Anne was trying not to face.

Susan wondered if she might scream a warning. A muffled scream inside the cabin wouldn't do; it would merely bring Steve hurrying to the cabin without putting him on guard. If she could get to the door, she might make him understand that they knew he was coming.

The door was behind her and to her right. She edged toward the end of the bench, estimating the steps she would have to take, planning to turn her back so she could reach the latch with her bound hands. Then Luke returned to the cabin, placed his hands on her shoulders again, and the chance was gone.

"Tanager's alone," Luke said to Anne. Susan couldn't be sure but she thought his fingers trembled slightly.

"There's no doubt of that. But he's smart and he's tough. I don't like dealing with him."

There was a wait; then Ernie Smith called from outside. Luke went to the door and scraped it open cautiously. There was more delay while Steve was blindfolded and tied. When he was brought into the cabin, he said, "Susan, are you here?"

"Yes, Steve." Her voice quavered a bit.

"Are you all right?"

"Yes," she said in a firmer tone. "I'm all right, Steve."

"You'd better be," he said to the room in general. "Are you blindfolded?"

"Yes."

"A lot of nonsense. Do these batterbrained idiots think we don't know who they are?"

"That blindfold could keep you alive," Luke said. His voice was less soft now. Susan wondered if he might be trying to disguise it.

Someone guided Steve to the bench, and he sat beside Susan with his back to the table so that they were facing in opposite directions. He whispered her name and pressed close to her. She lowered her head against his shoulder.

"The little lady has agreed to tell us where the money is if we share it with her," Luke said. "What do you think of that?"

"What I think doesn't seem to matter," Steve said.

"I don't trust you much, Major," Luke said. "The terms are agreeable to me provided I can be guaranteed against tricks, lies, and delays."

"You're dealing the cards."

"You're damn right we are," Ernie put in. "And we ain't forgetting Danny. You—"

"Shut up!" Luke snapped. "Let me think."

The pad of his boots came in measured cadence as he paced the floor. Steve's lips brushed Susan's cheek and he spoke softly into her ear.

"I was going to run out on you. I meant to get the money and skip," he said.

"But you didn't."

They found each other's lips and kissed briefly, warmly. Sitting there blindfolded and with her hands tied, they looked ridiculous to Ernie Smith, and he laughed.

"Shut up!" Luke was still pacing.

"Steve, play it safe," Susan said. "Do as they say. I want you to live. I don't want to live unless you do."

"Why, Mrs. Allison!" he said.

They kissed again, then she pushed away.

"I'm *not* Mrs. Allison, Steve. I never was anything except Mrs. Ben Roman."

Luke stopped pacing. For a moment there was no sound but the drum-roll of the rain on the cabin roof. Then Susan spoke softly, gravely, and as if there were no one to hear her but Steve.

"I told you that I was in Salt Lake City with my sister and brother-in-law when the news came that Ben had been hanged. At almost exactly the same time, I realized I was pregnant. We knew the letter telling my parents of my marriage had been held up by the snows and would be on the same stagecoach we took east. We knew that if we could get it, no one at home would have to know that I was Mrs. Roman. So I went home as Mrs. Ben Allison—a name we picked out of the air. We said my husband had been killed in a mining accident."

Steve pressed close to her, forgetting where they were and why, knowing only that they were together.

163

"Princess," he said.

"Touching," Luke said. "Very touching. Now we'll get down to business. First, I want to know exactly where that money is."

"We'll take you down there and show you," Steve said.

"I want to be told first. Right now, Major, without bargaining or stalling."

"It's in a hollow log in the cabin wall," Susan said.

Luke questioned her and she gave details. There was a brief silence while Luke seemed to be deciding on a plan.

"You and I will go down and get it, Major," he said finally. "The little lady will stay here with Anne and Ernie. She will be my insurance against tricks."

"There'll be no tricks," Steve said. "But if Susan is hurt—" The futility of making a threat came to him and he broke off. "All right. Untie me and let's be on our way."

"Outside," Luke said. "Ernie, step out here with us."

Steve stood up and Luke led him through the doorway into the wet night. The door slammed behind them.

"You can't get down that trail blindfolded, but you're going to have to manage it with your hands tied," Luke said. "I'm not trusting you one inch."

Ernie Smith chuckled softly.

"Be damned to both of you," Steve said.

"How long will it take us to get the money out of this log?" Luke said.

"Half an hour ought to do it."

"Good. Figure an hour to get there and back—maybe a little more. Ernie, is that watch of yours running?"

"Sure," Ernie said.

"Now I want you to hear this, Tanager, so you'll understand we're not playing games. Ernie, if I'm not back here in two hours, *kill the girl*. Don't fool around about it. Don't discuss it with Anne, just do it.''

"Sure. Wait two hours. Then do it."

Steve felt suddenly weak and sick. "Listen—"

"You listen, Major. I'm going to take off the blindfold now. You may get a bit of a shock."

"There'll be no shock," Steve said. "I'd know that voice anywhere."

# EIGHTEEN

Tim Gaul stationed himself where the stage road bent out of the main gulch and rose into the outskirts of town. He wore his buffalo coat. He carried his shotgun in one hand, a dark lantern in the other, a coil of rope over his shoulder, and he paced back and forth across the road. This was the post he had held on a wintry, long-ago night when his vigilantes had thrown a cordon around the town and had arrested every suspicious person in it.

Today he had spent his time as usual, shuttling between his cabin and the town. He had walked the street angry-eyed and sullen, resentful of everyone, yet not clearly understanding his resentment, associating it with incidents of eight years ago as much as with the failure of his vigilantes to rally when he called them last night. He had avoided Smiley Birk, who had never been a vigilante, and whom Tim considered an upstart. To Tim's way of thinking, Birk didn't count. It was Tim Gaul, the Angel of Wrath, who would give Star City the angry justice that would save it.

Then Riggs McClean had staggered out of the darkness and Tim had helped him to the sheriff's office. When

Riggs had been lifted to a cot and primed with whisky, had gasped his story, not much of it had registered with Tim except Anne Barabee's name. Anne Barabee—Luke Lumby's girl.

"Luke is back," Tim had mumbled. "He'll take over the town. Decent citizens—"

"Luke be damned!" Smiley Birk had said. "Tim, this is 1874! Think about today. You see anything interesting through that spyglass?"

Tim had seen the Tanagers walk from the hotel to the livery that morning. He had seen the buggy leave and had been misled by its trip up-gulch until he had caught sight of the major riding eastward alone, circling, keeping to the low places. Later, when the rain had let up, he had seen the major's arrival at Wiggins' cabin. He told Birk this.

"All right," Birk had said. "We'll have a quick look around town. Somebody might've seen which way that wagon headed. If not, we'll ride down to the flat."

"I'll need a horse," Tim had said.

"You stay here, Tim. Guard the town. Just don't shoot anybody."

Tim had disregarded the patronizing tone of these words and had fastened onto the phrase "guard the town." He had barged up the grade to his cabin, put on his buffalo coat, and got the rope and the lantern. When he got back to town, Birk and his men had left. Now, stolidly, he paced this familiar post where he could challenge all who traveled the stage road. And, in his mind, he was not alone but supported by a ring of vigilantes posted every hundred yards around the town.

Once, his sharp eyes caught a small motion in the shadow of an outlying shed. He bellowed a challenge and swung the bull's-eye of the lantern in that direction as a poncho-draped figure glided out of sight around the shed. Tim broke into an awkward, ambling run; but when he reached the shed he found nothing but a confusion of smallish boot prints.

The murdering cowards knew the jig was up, he thought as he returned to the road, and they were trying to sneak out of town. Well, precious few would make it. By dawn that galoot in the poncho would likely be hanging from a cottonwood or a corral gate.

For a time the night was quiet. No one traveled the road. Restlessness grew in Tim, and a nagging uncertainty. It was time for the signal to close in, time for the questioning, the trials, the executions . . .

The sudden rain startled him, almost brought him back to reality. Then two shots sounded somewhere down-gulch, and they were immediately followed by two more. About down on Union Flat, Tim figured. He remembered that Wiggins was down there—and the major. They were in something together. Wiggins had talked freely to the vigilantes once; he would talk again.

Tim jerked his head right and left, bellowing into the empty night for somebody to cover his post. Bending into his purposeful walk, the long buffalo coat flopping about him, he plunged down the road. Fifty yards away, a man in a poncho emerged from behind a woodpile and cautiously followed.

Tim was drenched with sweat as he wound through the tangled shadows and scattered ashen lights of the lower end of the flat, but the thought of shedding the buffalo coat didn't occur to him. He wondered briefly that the shots hadn't stirred up activity here; he had forgotten that the flat was peopled by foreigners who lived in fear of being involved in the troubles of a civilization they couldn't understand. He found Wiggins' cabin dark and empty. Light flickered feebly from the other cabin, and he headed for it. He approached haltingly, stepping to one side of the open door for a view of the interior. He saw Wiggins' long, supine figure and heard him muttering to himself.

Wiggins recognized him with pleading eyes. "Captain Gaul, you got to help me."

Tim hunkered down, opened the shutter on his lantern, and examined Wiggins' bandages. "Looks like the bleeding's stopped. Who shot you?"

"Major Tanager."

Tim nodded grimly. "Might've known. A bad one, that major."

"I want no more lies on my soul," Wiggins said mournfully. "It was a fair fight. I tried to shoot him in the back. He drew and got me."

Tim snorted his disgust. "Back-shooting tinhorn! You jumping well got what you deserved."

"I been wicked all my life," Wiggins sobbed. "I took three lives in my time, and I'll go to Hell. The first was a woman down in Central City. She was no good, but I didn't have to kill her . . ."

For a time, Tim was fascinated by the terrible confession Wiggins poured out. Then because there was no one else here to witness it, Tim grew restless. With the shotgun in hand, he strode to the door and looked helplessly across the rain-drenched flat. He couldn't remember how he happened to be alone here. Surely others would be along. Or would they?

A movement near a clump of sage off to his right caught his eye. He leaped from the doorway, cocked the shotgun, and aimed it.

"Come out with your hands up!" he roared. "Or

169

you'll get a quart of revolver balls!''

A man in a poncho rose slowly from behind the sage and stepped to one side. He held his hands high and was plainly terrified. It seemed to Tim that he might have seen the man before, but he didn't rightly place him.

"What in hell you doing out there?"

"I am Carlos Ramirez, *señor*. I suffer to say that I have been pursuing you."

"What you up to?"

Ramirez gestured futilely with his raised hands. "I tell the truth, *Señor* Gaul. I came to Star City to kill you. Tonight I have many chances. Only I cannot shoot."

Tim stared in disbelief. "Why you want to do that?"

"I am the brother of Miguel Ramirez."

"Who in hell is he?"

"Perhaps you remember him as 'Mexican Mike,' *señor*, for I am told he was called such here. You slaughtered him, *señor*."

Tim remembered, and the memory was distasteful. He lowered the shotgun, then jerked it up again.

"That was too bad," Tim said, "but it was his own fool fault. Me and my men only wanted to question him, but he opened fire on us. We blew him to pieces."

"I live in a remote village," Ramirez said, groping for words. "We did not hear from Miguel for many years. We thought he must be dead, but we could not be sure; so at last I came to look for him. The last we had heard from him was from Salt Lake City, and I went there. After much searching, I found a man who had known him and who knew how he died. So I came here—what do you say?—to make revenge for him. Only I could not shoot you, *Señor* Gaul. I have never shot a man."

Tim studied the man. Keeping the shotgun on him, he

moved close and extracted a revolver from a holster under the poncho.

"I have also a small pistol in my sleeve," Ramirez said. He lowered his arm and Tim gingerly removed the derringer.

"I reckon I got nothing against you," Tim said. "And I need a witness. You come inside and witness a man's confession."

They went into the cabin. Ramirez bent over Wiggins, laid a palm on his brow, and offered to go for a doctor. Tim seemed not to hear. He stood in the center of the cabin taking stock of the excavated floor, the single remaining log of the partition overhead, the pile of tools, the scattered logs and lumber.

"We'll hold the trial right here," he announced.

"A trial, *señor*?"

"Pick up some of those boards and lay them over here." Tim pointed to a place along the front wall of the cabin at the edge of a pit.

Knowing that he was a prisoner of a *loco*, Ramirez obeyed without question. Under Tim's supervision, he constructed a little platform of boards. When the work was finished, Tim stood in the doorway and stared impatiently across the flat toward the road. Three men weren't enough for a trial. Surely others were on their way. Or were they? He couldn't remember.

Ramirez bent over Wiggins, who whimpered that he was dying. He was sheet-white and soaked with sweat. Tim gave him a worried glance and turned back to the doorway.

"There's folks in those buildings down there," he said to Ramirez. "We'll fetch some of 'em up here, Mex. Let's go."

# NINETEEN

Luke Lumby reined to a stop fifty yards west of the cabin. He was leading the horse that carried Steve, whose hands were still lashed behind him. Now Luke dismounted and tethered both animals to a clump of sage. He motioned to Steve to get down.

"Everything better be exactly as you say it is, Major."

"I told you Wiggins is there," Steve said. "Dead by this time for all I know."

The rain slacked off to a niggling drizzle as they sloshed to the cabin door. Steve went in first. Wiggins started to speak; then, seeing with amazement that Steve was a prisoner and who his captor was, he for once held his tongue. Steve's eyes fell on the coil of rope that lay beside Wiggins, then on the rickety platform Ramirez had built.

Luke picked his way across the cabin to the treasure log, plainly marked by the saw cut near its end.

"Untie me, damn it," Steve said. "I'll give you a hand and we'll get the money and get out of here."

"I told you I'm not trusting you an inch farther than I have to," Luke said. "I can roll this thing out of the wall alone, and you stay tied. Back up against the wall there."

Luke made an inspection of the log, running his fingers along it affectionately. He found the small saw, slipped it into the cut, and went to work. He finished quickly, laid aside the saw, and seized the pick, intending to use it for a pry bar.

"Just turn around slow and raise your hands," Tim Gaul said from the doorway.

Luke turned. He hesitated, then dropped the pick and lifted his hands, knocking off his hat as if by accident.

"You, too, Major," Tim said.

Steve turned to show his tied hands. "I'm Mr. Lumby's prisoner."

Tim stepped slowly into the cabin, staring at Luke Lumby. Behind him, another figure came through the doorway, then others . . . There were eight or ten of them, shadowy men in sacklike blouses, short trousers, sandals. One wore a cone-shaped straw hat; others wore battered felt hats or were bareheaded. All dangled queues down their backs. They filed in, impassive except for an occasional frightened phrase in Cantonese, and they huddled into a corner near the door. Following them came Carlos Ramirez, carrying a lantern.

"Damn damnation, Tim!" Steve said. "What—"

Tim, who had been approaching Luke haltingly and wild-eyed, threw back his head and laughed raucously.

"Luke Lumby! The rat has shaved his whiskers—his head, too, by thunder! You think I wouldn't know you, man?"

With an abrupt, catlike motion he whisked Luke's revolver from its holster and slid it into a side pocket of the flopping buffalo coat.

"Tim, you listen to me," Steve said. "Susan's up on the north butte—Road Agents' Roost. She—"

"You'll get a chance to speak your piece at the trial," Tim said.

"Trial! Tim, there's no time to lose. She's up there with a dim-witted gun shark who'll kill her. For God's sake, cut me loose."

Tim seemed not to hear. He was jerking the shotgun right and left, keeping the whole room covered, barking at the Chinese to line up along the north wall. Ramirez was at Steve's elbow.

"He is a *perro rabioso, señor*, a mad dog. It is useless to protest."

"Untie me. Quick!" Steve presented his back and his bound hands to the Mexican. But Tim was upon them, waving the double muzzle of the shotgun in their faces, ordering Ramirez to one side.

Steve roared at him now. Tim jabbed him in the ribs with the shotgun and sent him staggering against the wall. Tim lined up the Chinese, addressing them as "citizens"; then he prodded Steve over beside Wiggins and made him sit down. Holding the cocked shotgun to Luke's head, fingers on both triggers, Tim forced him to lie prone while Ramirez tied him. When he was bound hand and foot, they dragged him over beside Steve and Wiggins, and Tim fixed the lantern on a pile of dirt so that its bull's-eye spotted the three men.

"Close the door, Mex," Tim said, climbing onto the platform. "This trial is now in session."

"Make a run for it!" Steve said to Ramirez. "Get the sheriff. He's down-gulch somewhere."

174

"I've got six revolver balls in each barrel," Tim said, patting his shotgun. "First man to make a break gets cut in two."

Ramirez met Steve's eyes and slowly shook his head. He cautiously closed the door and stepped away from it.

"This court represents the God-fearing citizens of this community," Tim asserted. "It's purpose is to deal with the murdering, thieving riffraff who have overrun us and organized against us . . ."

He ranted on, stomping and gesturing like a drunken actor. The lantern shone into Steve's eyes and made his head throb. In the dusk beyond the cone of light, the Chinese were a blurred, two-dimensional mass, passive and unreal. There would be no help from that quarter, Steve thought. These people were here against their will; they wanted only to get away without getting involved in something they didn't understand. Or did they understand? Resented, cheated, oppressed, they found a sort of armor in ignorance. But deep down, they understood, he decided. They sensed every force at work here. They understood perfectly.

". . . case of Slim Wiggins, who pleads guilty to murder," Tim was saying. "The court will now hear his confession."

Wiggins had apparently become oblivious to what was going on. He lay silent, eyes closed, beads of sweat glistening on his forehead. Tim stepped over and kicked the bottom of his boots.

"You want to save your soul from Hell? Speak up."

Wiggins looked around him in terror as he came fully awake. For a moment he struggled to speak without making a sound.

"How many men you killed?" Tim demanded.

". . . doctor, and a man of God . . ."

"Did you kill Jase Nooner? Tell the court what you told me a while ago! Confess, man, and save your soul."

"I killed him," Wiggins said feebly. "I took him for Tanager. One man looks like another standing in a window against the light. The major and me was both after Ben Roman's treasure . . ."

Wiggins rolled his head to stare in the direction of the treasure log. The coolies who stood in front of it shifted uneasily, as if to avoid the eyes of death.

"I wanted to deal with Mrs. Allison alone," Wiggins went on. "I knew that way station and about the room for married folks, so I knew which window to watch. I thought it was Tanager I'd got—till I got here and heard the talk . . ." His voice trailed away.

"That's all that's necessary!" Tim snapped. "He pleads guilty, and the duty of this court is clear. It sentences Slim Wiggins to hang by the neck until dead."

He spoke the last words slowly, relishing them. He swept the coil of rope up from the ground and tossed it toward Ramirez. "Cut that into two lengths, Mex." As he stepped back to the platform, he drew a hunting knive from somewhere within the buffalo coat and flung it at Ramirez' feet.

"We've got to make a break," Luke hissed. "This maniac will hang us all."

Steve didn't reply. His wrists were raw, his fingers numb, and a feeling of nightmare helplessness engulfed him. How long ago had they left the butte? An hour? Longer? How much more time did Susan have to live?

"Sit close," Luke said. "I'll try to untie your hands."

"No chance with this light on us," Steve said.

Tim beckoned to Ramirez, who brought him the two

lengths of rope. Tim dropped one, and with the shotgun in the crook of his arm, began to fashion a hangman's knot in the other.

"Next case is Luke Lumby. How does the prisoner plead?"

"The hell with you," Luke said.

"You deny you're Luke Lumby?"

"Never heard of him."

"You're known to this court to be Luke Lumby," Tim said. "You're a known road agent and murderer. Ben Roman confessed before he died, and he named you as his right-hand man. If you refuse to enter a plea, this court will consider that you plead guilty."

"What kind of justice is that?" Luke said.

"It's the justice of decent citizens who have given too much leeway to the scum of the earth! This court sentences you to hang by the neck until dead."

Tim finished the knot and tested its sliding action. He then tossed the rope up and over the log that had topped the cabin's partition. He picked up the other length of rope and began to make another noose.

"My God!" Luke said. "He means to do it right here."

"The condemned are entitled to a good drop," Tim announced. "Mex, you drag some of those loose logs over here. You!" He pointed at random to one of the Chinese. "Give him a hand."

At first the frightened man did not understand, or pretended not to; but when Tim stepped toward him with the shotgun leveled, he got to work in a hurry. The two men gathered the small logs torn from the partition and, following Tim's complicated instructions, laid them into a sort of truncated pyramid. This had two boards inserted into it endways at a steep angle, and it seemed a crack-brained conception. Then Steve saw that it was a diabolically ingenious one. A strong shove on the ends of the boards would send the whole pile of logs rolling. If a man were standing on it with a noose around his neck . . .

Steve got painfully to his feet, and with a show of respect for the "court," tried to drive it home to Tim that he had to get out of there, that Susan's life was at stake. Tim simply didn't hear. He busied himself overseeing Ramirez and the Chinese; now and again he squarely turned his back. When Steve walked close and shouted into his ear, Tim forced him back to his place with cruel jabs of the shotgun and made him sit down.

Tim tossed the second noose over the beam above them. "Bring the condemned forward, Mex—you and the China-boy. Lumby first."

Ramirez hesitated, then seemed to reach a decision and made no protest. He approached Luke and bent over him, standing squarely behind Steve. The bite of the hunting knife was swift and clean as it slashed through the rope that bound Steve's hands.

"*Los Chinos a la izquierda, señor,*" Ramirez said in his native tongue. "They have maneuvered a log from the wall."

The words made no sense for a moment; then Steve turned his head and saw that they were true. The Chinese behind him and to his left now stood in front of an empty black space in the wall. They had seen the saw cut perhaps; anyway, they had discovered that the log could be worked loose. Instinctively grasping at any possibility of escape, they had pushed it outward from the wall.

Luke was twisting, butting, driving his heels into the ground as Ramirez and the Chinese tried, halfheartedly, to drag him forward. Tim stood on the piled logs, his shotgun

178

carelessly propped against his stomach as he deftly secured a rope to the beam.

Knowing clearly now what he must do, Steve again got to his feet. The simple way to avoid Tim's attention was to try to focus it on something his crippled mind couldn't bear to face.

"If it please the court," Steve said, "I'd like to ask a question."

"Ask it."

"Am I on trial, too?"

Tim gave him a brief scowl—as if trying to remember who he was. "Not yet. When the executions are over, we want the answers to some questions. In the meantime, you're a prisoner of this court."

"May I remind the court that this is the year 1874?" Steve said. "May I point out that it has been eight years since the execution of Ben Roman? . . ."

For an instant, Tim looked as if he had been struck; then he turned away. He stepped down from the logs and gave his attention to the matter of bringing Luke forward, helping Ramirez and the Chinese lift him onto the logs.

Steve moved casually to the left, picking his way around the excavation below the dangling ropes. He kept talking, saying what he knew Tim couldn't bear to hear.

"There are county courts now and elected officers . . ."

Luke stood on the pile of logs now, held up by Ramirez and the Chinese. He hurled curses down on Tim.

"You're a kill-crazy strangler, Gaul!" he shouted. "You always were! You and Bill Illingsley! Well, I did for Illingsley, old man. I want you to know that. I killed him and I'm proud of it!"

Steve stepped backward toward the gap in the wall. The Chinese in front of it slid to one side. Tim climbed up beside Luke and the two stood eye to eye. Luke was still shouting. Tim reached for the noose.

Steve bent into the opening, shoving his head and shoulders through, flattening his body into it and sliding into the fresh night air. He stumbled into the treasure log, got his feet under him, and raced toward the horses Luke had tied off to the west. Dodging around sagebrush, bending low, he expected any moment to hear the shotgun blast that would tear life out of him. But it didn't come. When he reached the horses, he glanced back and saw that no one had come out of the cabin. Intent on ignoring any truth that threatened his world of madness, Tim apparently hadn't even missed him yet.

# TWENTY

The rain had stopped when Steve reached the butte, and the moon slid brightly across a crevice in the clouds. He urged his horse recklessly up the treacherous trail, left the animal, began the last, breath-taking part of the climb. This seemed the ultimate ordeal that his sanity could endure. He knew that almost an hour must have been used up in travel to the flat and back; he had no idea how long he had spent as Tim Gaul's prisoner. If a shot were to ring out in the pines above him now, he thought, there would be nothing left of him but madness as hopeless and as deadly as Gaul's.

At the top of the climb he seized a sledge-size piece of rock and staggered into the pines. He reached the cabin door and, holding his rasping breath, paused to listen. At first he heard nothing at all; then he made out a faint, familiar click of playing cards. Someone was passing the time at solitaire. Praying that it was Ernie Smith, he put his shoulder to the door and threw himself into the room, the rock in his raised right hand.

Susan and Anne sat at the table with their backs to the door. Ernie sat across from them with the cards laid out in front of him, a watch and a gun at his right. Steve hurled the rock. It missed Ernie's head by six inches, forcing him to dodge and spoiling his grab for the gun. Steve reached the end of the table and tipped it toward Ernie, turning the candle into his face, spilling him backward off the bench.

Now Steve found himself in the dark, in a tangle of moving furniture. His shin hit the edge of the bench painfully. He stumbled into Ernie, who was bouncing to his feet with amazing agility and who had another gun—the one he had taken from Steve. The weapon thundered its stab of flame past Steve's head; burning powder stung his face and neck. He grabbed at the flash, caught the gun hand, flung it upward as the gun roared again, wrenched the elbow forward, and felt the arm break as Ernie pitched over his hip.

He raked a match across his rump and saw Ernie on his back, grasping his torn arm, the fight gone out of him. Steve picked up a gun, kicked a second out of reach, picked up the candle, and touched the match to it. His ears were ringing from the gunshots, and Anne Barabee's voice was oddly muffled.

"Luke's dead," she said. "You don't need to say it. I know he's dead."

He expected to see agony in her face but found only resignation. He didn't know how to answer her, and he put down the candle and turned to Susan. He removed her blindfold, then untied her hands and took her into his arms.

"I know he's dead," Anne said again, "and I'm glad. Do you hear me? I'm glad!"

"I'm going to leave you here with Ernie," Steve said

curtly. "The sheriff will be along sometime before daylight. There's no sense in trying to get away."

Fan-tan Flat was an unreal place of glistening moonlight and grave-black shadows. Saddlehorses drooped in front of the treasure cabin. As Steve and Susan rode up, a figure slid into the bright rectangle of the doorway. It was Ramirez, and he stepped out to meet them.

"I have brought the sheriff, *señor*," he said as he caught the head of Steve's horse. "I found him in the lower gulch as you suggested."

Another man, one of Birk's deputies, stepped out of the shadows. "Look who's here," he said.

Steve dismounted and motioned to Ramirez to hold Susan's horse. "Stay with her, Carlos. She mustn't see what's inside."

He moved swiftly to the doorway and stopped there. Tim Gaul sat on a log in the glare of the lantern, the buffalo coat draped loosely around him. Smiley Birk and a deputy stood over him, glaring, waiting for him to speak. Birk had taken Tim's shotgun and he held it in the crook of his arm. Beyond them, swaying ever so slightly, two bodies hung puppet-like with their heads twisted grotesquely.

"All right, Tim!" Birk said. "Suppose that *is* Luke Lumby up there. Suppose I take your word for it till I know different. What about the other one—the tinhorn? Why in the black damnation did you string him up?"

"He—killed—Jase Nooner," Tim said. The harsh, commanding voice was gone; the words came slowly and feebly. "He gave us—a proper confession."

Steve stepped on into the cabin, and Birk swore mightily when he saw him.

"We haven't found your wife," Birk said. "We found a wagon and an empty trunk a ways off the road. We figure—"

He broke off, staring open-mouthed at Susan, who had come into the doorway, Ramirez tugging ineffectually at her sleeve. She gaped briefly at the hanging figures, then covered her face with her hands.

Steve strode to her and tried to lead her away; but before he could do so, she looked again and pointed in amazement at the body suspended beside Wiggins'.

"That's— Why, that's the man at the poker table that night in Ogden—"

Steve nodded. "Chancey Duncan, we called him. But he was Luke Lumby, and at heart he was the killer he had always been."

She leaned heavily against him as he led her toward the horses. Smiley Birk followed them closely.

"He told me a little about himself on the way down here," Steve said. "After he left here eight years ago, he came down with typhoid, and it left him bald. He also shaved his fancy beard, which had become sort of a trademark. And eight years is a long time. He and Wiggins didn't know each other when they met in Ogden. Luke didn't even recognize you at first. But as luck would have it, his room was next to yours. He listened at the wall and made out who you were and what you were up to. He rounded up Daniels and Ernie Smith—and you know the rest. They took an old freight road and a Bannock trail and beat Wiggins up here by a few hours . . ."

"Did you know he was Luke Lumby?" Susan said. "Before you saw him, I mean."

"When Anne made it plain that she knew we weren't married, I began to wonder. Chancey was the only person who knew that and also knew we were working with Wiggins. I could make that add up only one way.''

Birk asked his thousand questions then, and he sent his deputies after Anne and Ernie. In little more than an hour they were back, having picked up the wagon, too.

Steve and Susan rode off toward town but circled back and halted behind the other cabin, in the shadow of the spur. They waited till the wagon lumbered off, loaded with Anne, Ernie Smith, Ramirez, Tim Gaul, and the two dead men, and escorted by Birk and his deputies. When it reached the stage road, Steve urged his horse across the silent flat, and Susan followed.

They rode to the rear of the treasure cabin, where the treasure log should have been lying below the gap in the wall—and wasn't.

Steve leaped down from the saddle, struck a match, and examined the ground. Dozens of sandal prints covered the area.

"The Chinese!" he said.

Susan stared down at him dumbfounded.

"They got it," he said. "The whole damn logful of it!"

She slid down beside him, moaning, staring at the tracks, following them with her eyes toward the dismal maze of buildings at the lower end of the flat.

"They understood about the treasure," Steve said. "They were watching, waiting a chance at it. Tim Gaul gave it to them. They pushed the log out of the wall. When he let them leave, they simply took it with them."

"Is there—anything—we can do?" Susan asked thinly.

They both knew there wasn't. By now that log was hacked into a dozen pieces, burning in a dozen fires. The money was secreted in a dozen undiscoverable hiding places.

"Sometimes you lose," Steve said.

Susan threw back her head, and there was more than a touch of hysteria in her laugh. She quickly controlled it and said, "In a way, the community got it, after all!"

And so they stood in the wet and shimmering barrenness of Fan-tan Flat, this star-scarred gambler and the woman he called his princess. Their eyes met and she came into his arms.

He said, "We'll be all right, Susan—together."

"Together," she said.

## ROUND UP THESE WESTERNS
## FROM BERKLEY PUBLISHING CORP.!

GUNPOINT                        (03400-3—$1.25)
   by William O. Turner

MAYBERLY'S KILL            (03454-2—$1.25)
   by William O. Turner

MONTANA PASSAGE         (03096-2—$ .95)
   by Allan Vaughan Elston

POSSE OF KILLERS            (03276-0—$1.25)
   by Sam Victor

THE RUTHLESS RANGE       (03333-3—$1.25)
   by Lewis B. Patten

SHORTCUT TO DEVIL'S CLAW   (03410-0—$1.25)
   by William O. Turner

TRAIL OF VENGEANCE       (03461-5—$1.25)
   by Louis Kretschman

---

Send for a *free* list of all our books in print

---

These books are available at your local bookstore, or send
price indicated plus 30¢ per copy to cover mailing costs to
Berkley Publishing Corporation
390 Murray Hill Parkway
East Rutherford, New Jersey 07073